D0098044

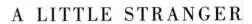

A LITTLE STRANGER

By Candia McWilliam

A LITTLE STRANGER
A CASE OF KNIVES

DOUBLEDAY

NEW YORK · LONDON · TORONTO · SYDNEY · AUCKLAND

A
LITTLE
STRANGER

Candia McWilliam

PUBLISHED BY DOUBLEDAY,
a division of Bantam Doubleday Dell Publishing Group, Inc.
666 Fifth Avenue, New York, New York 10103

DOUBLEDAY and the portrayal of an anchor
with a dolphin are trademarks of Doubleday,
a division of Bantam Doubleday Dell
Publishing Group, Inc.

All of the characters in this book are fictitious,
and any resemblance to actual persons, living or
dead, is purely coincidental

Design by Richard Oriolo

Library of Congress Cataloging-in-Publication Data applied for

ISBN 0-385-26309-0
Copyright © 1989 by Candia McWilliam
All Rights Reserved

Printed in the United States of America

July 1989

First Edition in the United States of America

BG

There lies that solid world
These hands can never reach;
My history, my love,
Is but a choice of speech.

A terror shakes my tree,
A flock of words fly out,
Whereat a laughter shakes
The busy and devout.

Wild images, comes down
Out of your freezing sky,
That I, like shorter men,
May get my joke and die.

"Trinculo's Song"
W. H. AUDEN

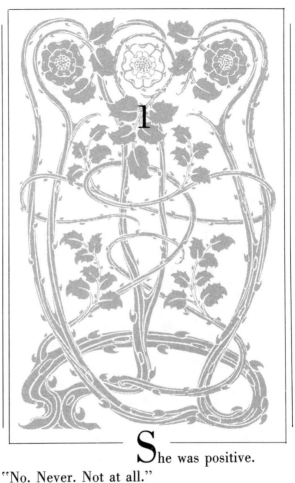

1

She was positive.

"No. Never. Not at all."

"And boyfriends? Or do you have someone in particular?"

She put her small hand up to her short neck, took

strength from the goffered angora she found there to fortify her against my too-direct question, and spoke.

"I am engaged."

I imagined the lock on an old-fashioned lavatory giving the same information, with similar blankness. But I do not mean to suggest she was vacant. I was pleased to observe her behaviour. I had always believed that simple people have more hope of virtue, not plotting to attain it in the complicated ways of the faulty and sophisticated.

"You don't wear a ring?"

"I don't wear jewellery for work. It can scratch the little skins." She made of children grapes, easily popped out of their plumpy skins.

I felt raisin-like myself that day, and very much older than the young woman whom I was interviewing for the post of nanny to my son.

She looked quite at ease in the tall pale room, but she was keeping her personality within the space she occupied physically. It was my room, filled with my books, my flowers, my way of being, into which she had not so much fitted as inserted herself, neatly, not in parenthesis but clearly marked by the pointed caret provided by her scent. It was a smell of blossom and powder, not pungent but very strong. It was as chemically pink as the wad of filling in a sweet biscuit.

For lunch I had eaten approximately seventy black

2

olives, of the type which is wrinkled and black as tar on a summer road. I accompanied them with a jug of black coffee. My back teeth were sandy with its grounds. The girl had refused coffee or tea, saying she drank no stimulants.

"None? Ever?" I had asked, receiving that vehement triple negative, of which she was so certain. "No. Never. Not at all." She said that she and the boy—he was her age, twenty-two—would marry when they had saved for a house. He worked with animals, she said. She told me her father was a policeman, her mother a part-time teacher. It might be said that Solomon, my husband, also works with animals.

He was not usually able to come home in the middle of the day, though he did not have to go far for his work. Most days I ate a plateful of something he disliked for lunch, so we could share the sort of food —good plain food—he wanted for dinner. I would read at the same time as I ate, but never the periodicals which my husband might want to read in case they got spattered with smoked roes or raw steak or the vinegar of capers. Sometimes I even managed to find the gelatinous pinkish herring, *"haring,"* of my Dutch childhood. John would find me out at once. "Like kissing a seal," he would say. Our child ate separately, real food of a nourishing and unsubtly appetising nature. His palate was too clean for the

3

food I favoured. But his old nanny, who had kept his plate bright with planks of fish and discs of carrot and bright green peas, was going, and I must find a successor.

I could see nothing wrong with this girl. She was the first applicant for the job who was pretty. Children notice appearances. Her references were excellent and she had brought with her a small valise of toys and projects she had made for her last charges, of whom she also brought photographs. They appeared well maintained and happy.

She was a country girl, she said, so she would not be lonely in this house. We lived at the heart of possessed lush land, not near anywhere, a large working estate flanked by others.

"There are nannies all around," I said. It was true. Just here, at this prosperous country's rich core, children came like the seasons, annual, beautiful, and wanted in their time. Some of our neighbours had six children, none fewer than three. I, with just our son, was only beginning. The nannies came and went, their importance inexaggerable. All these children lived at a nannied remove from their parents. It kept both children and parents younger than their years. The benediction bestowed by money was to be seen all about. It was unquestioned as the fresh air.

Her name was Margaret Pride. She had become a nanny because she loved children, all children. I did not ask why, in that case, she had not become a nurse, to look after those children who need extra care, children not just less fortunate than my son, but also sick. There are people who cannot bear illness, seeing it as a weakness. She was short and I guessed that she had trouble with her figure. She had the round wrists and belted midriff of one who has trouble shifting the puppy fat which makes young women appear middle-aged before time. She had a clean look and was unexceptionally dressed, something I do not find easy to achieve. She looked as though she would be able to enter a chain store and select a co-ordinated outfit, and then only when her building society account would stand it. Over her angora piecrust-necked jersey she wore a suit jacket, teamed with its skirt, both the pale green of sherbet limes. Her shoes and handbag were the pale yellow-grey of destroyers seen from afar. They were of a style too old for her. The bag closed with the short locked tusks of a graminivore. Her legs ended in feet; there were no ankles.

"I'm perfectly happy for you to wear jeans," I said. She turned her head and gave no grin at the incongruity of a woman only a few years older than herself and dressed as a scarecrow telling her she might dress casually.

"I prefer to be neat," she said. She implied no criticism of my appearance. It was as though she

5

accepted that my position as mother of her source of income, wife of her source of payment, gave me licence to dress as I pleased. I dressed as an ex-beauty, though it was not clear to me whether this was appreciated by others. I wore that day, as I almost always did by then, a pair of men's jeans, a huge jersey and trodden-down party shoes. My dressing-room was full of duplications of this uniform.

"I would be perfectly happy to wear a uniform," she said.

"I don't think we need go that far," I replied, and made a face whose message was that I would never impose the sort of behaviour that implied on anybody. "But there is one thing I do mind about," I continued. I wanted to tell her I did not like her scent, but I didn't have the stomach to say it.

"Yes?" she enquired.

A little disarmed by her eagerness to please, I became confiding. "I may not look it, but I am fanatically tidy, about drawers and clothes and food and the nursery and so on. Sort of the opposite to a whited sepulchre, I suppose; something like a blackened basinette, or a . . ." Sometimes I talked too much, not having spoken to anyone for a time. When I did talk to people, they were frequently the wrong ones. I was abuzz with words, which would not always swarm about their proper hive. I was not often alone but I was never precisely more than accompanied.

Margaret gave a warm, calming smile. "Some people," she responded, "have said I am too tidy myself. I find it satisfying to see everything in its place. And I love lovely things. I'm like that."

"Would you like to see the nursery part of the house?" I asked. I wanted to please her. "Leave your bag, it'll be fine." She left it, rather reluctantly.

We went up the front stairs; the back stairs were those our child and his nanny always used. Everything was white and blue and tall. The hallways smelt of flowers and no dust. On the walls were pictures, at which she did not look. Although the child's voice was audible, she did not follow it. I found it hard not to go to him when I heard his voice. We went on upstairs and into the room which might be hers. It looked out over fat, green fields which swelled under the July heat. The grey tower of the church showed among shimmering crowns of trees. The room was full of light and pleasantly furnished with a green-painted wooden bed, a curtained wash basin, two tables, a television, a sofa. It was decorated with a sad, pretty chintz, as though for a maiden daughter.

She came to no spoken judgement. I took her to the nursery kitchen where the nanny cooked her own food and the child's and where other children and nannies were entertained. The smocked curtains moved at the bright window, from which the formal garden was visible, its hedges enclosing rain-clouds of grey lavender. She looked around like someone wondering whether or not to buy, and again said nothing. Sensible, really, not to be beguiled by things. After all, the child was the point. In "her" sitting-room and the nursery bathroom she also passed no remark. She must perhaps be shy. Her last job had been in much the same sort of place, but perhaps I intimidated her. I am told I can. I am taller than most and have more hair. I also look at other people very hard. In the nursery bathroom, she said, "Where do you change?"

I could not understand the question at first. Did she think I was a werewolf?

"Nappies," she explained.

"He's out of them," I said.

"For a baby." She was unblushing. This really did disconcert me.

"Do you have a baby up your sleeve?" I asked, making light of her shawled question.

"I am sure you will have another," she said, and the sense that she was accustomed to command made me leave her to her certainty, for the moment.

In John's room, she looked around, standing in the room's dead centre, as though the round blue nursery rug were a little pond and she a solid

"Grace" in the middle. He played at the rim of the rug, angling for glances from me and his nanny. He had the stagy concentration of a pampered cat watching goldfish, neck bent, eyes down, nerves rehearsing real hunger. When Margaret and I came in, he and his nanny had been together on the floor; now she was in a corner of the room, folding white squares as though for a mass surrender.

John waited to hear the stranger speak.

"Cat got your tongue?" asked Margaret. He looked up. Her smile was all dimples and comfort. He flopped towards her on the blue, just a child again, his fair head in his hands and the bare soles of his feet waving, in the immemorial pose of a boy whose attention has been hooked.

Later, I went downstairs, leaving her to get to know the child. After a time the nanny who was about to leave came down and we sat in the kitchen. She liked black coffee too. I liked her, but she was leaving to be married, and was sorry to go, so I did not make it harder for her by talking about her departure. She was a sensible girl who made things with her hands and enjoyed masochistic sports—potholing, freefalling and such. I had even worked a little while she was with us, though I listened too much for the child.

"What do you think?" I asked.

"She brought a packet of sweets for him," she said. "So he thinks she's great."

She is bound to be jealous, it's a difficult time, I thought.

I said, and felt disproportionately disloyal as I did so, "Do you approve?"

"Not of sweets," said the girl who was to depart, knowing that a part of her life was coming to an end, the important part just beginning.

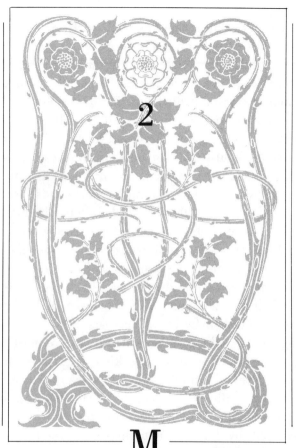

2

Margaret Pride came to
live with us and to look after our child. My husband
was especially pleased. "She's smartly turned out,"
he said. I thought of a jelly, arriving entire on the
dish from its mould, not a curve out of place, sweetly

buttressed. John seemed to love her. He was an easy boy, with no temper and a desire to please. He was curious and affectionate and big for his age. He had astonishing looks which caused people to talk to whomever accompanied him in the street. He had brown eyes and white hair and he fell over often because his feet were large and he thought most of the time about private matters. He was a little timorous, and easily shamed. He did not like to be laughed at. He enjoyed bringing new words into his vocabulary, where they would be altered by his lisp and his accent, which combined the country voices of his familiars—cook, nannies, gardeners and so on—with the vowels of his parents and our friends. He also had a trick of substituting f for v, as in "ferry nice." It was as though his grandparental Dutchness was coming out. Excellent linguists, they yet trip on English v's and w's. Where the idioms are most contiguous, the Dutchman speaking English is most likely to reveal himself. Asked how many peas are in a pod, he will reply, "Ten, of so" for "ten, or so." Margaret's standard English was the off-white kind favoured by hotel receptionists and vendeuses of posh slap.

John's fourth birthday fell in the first week of Margaret's employment, also, coincidentally, the beginning of the grouse season. John was gun-shy so far, and I did not want to go north in Margaret's first

12

weeks, so he, she and I were living in the house. She did not use my Christian name. On the whole I found this an advantage.

John had spoken to his father on the telephone on the eve of his birthday. I had kissed him goodnight; his hair smelled of puppies and milky tea, sweet and smoky, the scent of toy-gun caps held in a soaped hand. Margaret was present during both John's valedictions to his parents that evening.

She had a position for waiting, which was suggestive of the not sufficiently swift passage of time. She would turn and turn a lock of her own hair, having isolated it from the soft moss standing over her forehead, and turn her right foot over too, so its ankle, or rather leg, touched the ground. Her invariably high heel would in this way be turned inwards like a spur.

Certainly, she drove herself. The buzz of her activity filled the house. She got up early and did laundry and ironing until very late. I knew these things because I listened. Big houses carry sound as water does; the sound is clarified by the space. But she was also quite unmuffled in her activity. Her shoes tapped her presence. She behaved as though I suspected her of sneaking off for a lie-down or a cigarette, and would tell me what she had been and what she intended doing. "I've just done the ironing and I'm off to sort through the toys."

"Don't take on too much," I had said to her.

"Only do John's stuff, and please tell me if any-thing's not right, if anything doesn't suit. I can't always guess everything."

I had not guessed anything when she surprised me in the nursery kitchen that evening. I had made him a tree, composed of sweets. The trunk was of flaky logs of chocolate, and the leaves and fruits were boiled sweets in twists of coloured paper. My idea was that he would be allowed one sweet after lunch each day until it was finished. By that time it would be autumn.

I was putting his tree beside his place at the nurs-ery table, which Margaret had already laid for break-fast. She was good at thinking ahead. Events did not catch her out. She kept a collapsible umbrella in the back of the car. When it rained she wore a hood of transparent plastic. After the morning walk she al-ways cleaned her gumboots. They put ours to shame. Hers were small and black and shiny. Like all her possessions, they were marked with her name, "M. Pride." Such items as her hairbrush, difficult to label, she had identified with pink nail varnish, "M.P." She favoured babyish objects of adult neces-sity: a vanity case with a teddy bear upon it, an elec-tric toothbrush in the shape of a chipmunk, bedroom slippers whose toes were the masks of mice, with grey crewel whiskers. These things were also named, although they could only have been hers.

I was looking about the nursery kitchen, happy with what I saw. Margaret was as orderly as she had claimed to be and as I had stipulated. Nothing was out of place, nothing missing. It was surely in such a rational and ordered state that John's spirit would grow confident and free, untroubled by chaos.

"Just before I do this little lot," came the voice of Margaret, accompanied presently by her body, hugging a red plastic basket of clothes, and wrapped in an apron. The apron enquired, "Have you hugged someone today?"

"Yes?" I asked, pleased that she was perhaps about somewhat to fill the hours ahead, maybe with talk of John. I would not have minded contact rather greater than we had. After all, the child was a very personal conduit for conversation. I did not want her to tell me her hopes and fears. I would not tell her mine. Surely we could discuss the boy without danger.

I also wanted to know that she was all right in order to ascertain for how long she might consider staying. If only she could stay for the whole of John's small boyhood.

"I just wondered. That is, I wonder if we might have a piece of garden?" she asked.

"We?"

"John and I. He has an interest in growing things. I would make sure he did not tread dirt inside."

"What a marvellous idea. I'm only sorry I didn't think of it before. Where do you think?"

"I asked Daddy" (she referred thus to my husband) "and Mount" (our gardener) "before He went up to Scotland." The *h* was capitalised so that I knew it was of my omnipotent husband that she spoke. Who was our son, if Solomon was God? Little Sol, the Sun of man.

I flinched from asking myself whether I felt jealous, and of whom.

I thought of something. "Do you believe in God?" I asked, having forgotten to ask this at the interview. Should I have been so flustered?

"I believe that things are meant, and my father is a lay reader," she replied, putting the basket down upon the polished oxblood floor and looking at me as though I had used strong language against her. She wore a crucifix too small to martyr anything but a fly. I recollected what we had been discussing.

"Back to the garden," I said. "John's, not Eden."

I did not, as one is supposed to, grow better at judging an audience as I grew older.

"I thought," and her voice went from discomfiture to satisfaction as she spoke, "that we'd start with radishes and marigolds, bright and quick-growing."

"And, how nice, both edible," I said, my voice rather too social in my ears. It really was a lovely idea. I imagined John pulling up his first radish, that

16

unearthly pink with its creamy puzzle. We could make radish sandwiches and marigold salad and give a little—what else?—garden party.

"Edible?" said Margaret. "Marigolds?"

"Delectable in salads." Delectable? Handy hints for cross-cultural cuisinastes. "Just scattered. Not too thickly." I was losing confidence. "The petals only."

"Everything in its place," said Margaret. "We don't want him eating laburnum pods for peas. I know how unsettling foreign things can be." Sensibly, I felt, she had tried out these foreign things and found them wanting. One could only pity Pascal, Descartes and those old Greeks with beards and unironed drapes.

"No, of course we don't. How right you are."

"We thought by the thornless blackberries, well away from the glasshouses and frames."

"It's a wonderful idea, Margaret. Why don't you get cracking in the morning? John would adore it. How are you settling in, by the way, yourself? What about anything you need?"

"I've everything I need," she said. "There's a programme I fancy in a while and I've got to put these garments in, so I'll say goodnight."

"Goodnight," I said. "God bless you." Who was I, to invoke Him? It was another bit of social speech.

I spent the evening, after a supper of sweetbreads and rye bread, reading. I could not see that there was much on television but serials about the effects of illness or of wealth. I could not differentiate between these programmes, though the outfits worn by the victims sometimes gave a hint, and the terminally ill, or those who impersonated them, appeared to wear even more make-up than the terminally rich.

I was reading and correcting the proofs of a book. It was the author of the book who was doing me a favour, not I him. I did not need the work, rather the idea that I had it. This particular author could not write but could not help selling. The book was intended to be bought rather than read; it was a category book of gossip, easier to write than a bird book or a tree book and less resistible. People have no certain profile in flight and no certain season of falling sap, so research need not be exhaustive.

When my eyes were tired, I went out into the garden through the back door. The sky was quite light still and the flowers no longer bright, but incandescent. Only one particularly scarlet rose had not softened in shade. The flowers glowed like candles behind guards of coloured vellum.

The house stood, a substantial cube among its blue lawns. Within it my son slept, needing nothing I could give him. My husband was far from home.

Light fell from Margaret's window. At its edge a curtain moved, then swept across, a thin wave lipped with lace at its rim. Mist filled the lower air, lapping at my knees. I stood outside, alone, at the margin of house and park.

A green star fell. Perhaps I could make solid the expressed desire of my husband and Margaret by conceiving a child. There I would be, with my children, the keystone of the family monument.

There was rain in the air. I did not feel it a threat. I knew that I held, with my husband, the umbrella of family love which will keep out even the most terrible rain.

I followed the path behind two lead hinds and turned left beyond the lily tank, through a gate and into the kitchen garden. The red whips of the thornless blackberries made a Pompeian arch against the grey wall, which bounded a most dapper bit of hoeing about five feet square.

A small clean rake and spade and a duck-shaped watering can stood in a green wheelbarrow which reached only to my calves. The barrow was parcelled like an expensive bouquet in cellophane. A clearly written label within, in writing not my husband's read, "To John with fond regards from 'Daddy.'" It was from Margaret's own writing pad, whose paper was headed "Love is a warm feeling inside." I felt cold. Along the bottom of the paper walked, in disciplined manner, two ducks and their fluffy duckling.

She must have been sure of the weather. It was not like her to enterprise the god of rain.

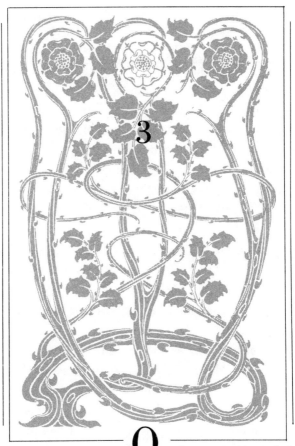

On the morning of his birthday, John ate most of his tree of sweets before breakfast. How could he know that the sweets were for serial plucking? He was not sick, but he did no justice to his executed egg with its squad of toast soldiers.

Since it was John's day, he could not be in disgrace, so I put myself there in his stead and said to Margaret, "I'm sorry. It was thoughtless of me."

"It's the thought that counts," she said, pulling in her stomach and at the same time smoothing the small of her back, as though wiping off chalk dust like an old-fashioned school-mistress.

I felt gratitude at the mildness of her rebuke. I didn't think to ask her why she had allowed John to eat the sweets. She had given him her present, a selection of bright seed packets.

"Must need see garden any minute, Mum," announced my son.

"Mummy," said Margaret.

"Yes?" I responded facetiously, and the little joke died.

We went to John's new garden. I had arisen even earlier than Margaret, whose rising was marked by the roaring of machines for washing and for drying clothes. Around the necks of the leaden hinds, I had twisted flowers taken from the border I had patrolled by dusk the previous night. The hinds were bloomed with a dust like talc, more opaque in the creases of the soft metal.

"Oh how nice. See what the fairies have done," said Margaret. The hollyhocks and morning glories

22

at once looked silly to me, whimsical and fey, like a unicorn at Pony Club.

John marched on past the water-lily tank. The water was green as bottle-glass. Margaret held him very tight. "It only takes three inches of water for them to *d-r-o-w-n,*" she said, spelling out the letters of the frightening word, though she was not walking between the child and the tank but between him and the wall, which was pinned with climbing plants. The tank was at least twenty feet deep, after the ten-foot drop.

John's garden was a success. He scattered some seeds from Margaret's packets and was only a little disappointed when nothing sprang up at once.

"Slowly slowly catchee monkey," he said, nodding heavily. He was being Mount.

He watered his garden. The backs of his legs were still fat. He did not yet show the double tendons which web the backs of older boys' knees. John was like an egg, round and whole.

When he had finished watering his garden, he washed his tools at the garden tap—the smell of earth and water calling up autumn—and said, "What does dear are oh double you hen mean, Margaret?"

"What you've just done to your garden," almost-interrupted Margaret, and tapped his bottom, not hard, with her hand. The cushion of love at the base of her thumb was soft like the foot of a baby.

It was a happy day and, at tea, when John said, "Margaret stay with me always not ever leaving," I agreed with him aloud and in my heart. I was sad that he already knew what leaving meant.

"I'll drink to that," said Margaret, lifting her glass of chocolate milk to her lips. She looked pretty today, nice for John to look at. I had given up all thought of complaining about her scent. She was wearing a modest and becoming frock, daintily embroidered at neck and hem with dancing people. Its belt was narrow and almost leather, like the collar of a realistic toy dog.

Later, I spoke to my husband on the telephone.

"Margaret settling in?" he asked. "Are you doing all you can for her?"

"Yes. And what a lovely idea the garden was. He is delighted. He loves the small wheelbarrow. You chose well."

His voice, always distant, sounded yet further away, a trick he had when he chose not to go in for unnecessary explanations, as though he had with difficulty remembered some tiresome but not urgent pieces of business.

"Still toiling away at the galleys?" he asked, courteously acknowledging my sham work.

"Still potting away at the enemy?" I asked, not so courteously riling him for his sham warfare.

"Getting tricksy without me, I see." He sounded amiable. "Time for a new addition, and I'm meaning that with an *a*. Margaret would like that. A little stranger for us all. Goodnight, love."

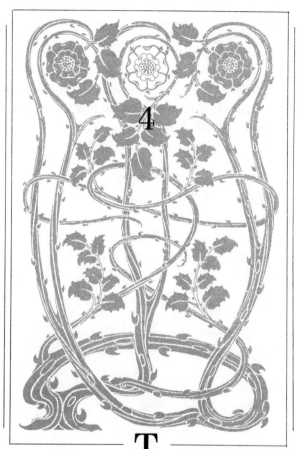

The house as a perfectible
ideal of civilised activity is a less exclusive idea than
it has even been. We visit the palaces of the collector-
dukes and bachelor connoisseurs, not only for what
we may learn of history and beauty, but for what we

may borrow and apply to our own houses. The dwellings of artisans, too, are displayed, and we are invited to observe how stylish was their way with simple materials. We take this innocent style and in embracing it bring it to consciousness. We travel through rooms no longer private and imagine we understand the past, when all we have seen is a varnished plaster suckling pig slowly turning between electrically cranked firedogs. We are ravished by our own ability to save labour and the ability of the dead households to employ and deploy it. And there is money; we feed on the loveliness it has sheltered, deaf to the rolling thud of its demolishing ball, held high over us on a frail chain by a rusting crane.

When one small cushion, embroidered with silk fine as eyelash to resemble a corner of chrysanthemine meadow, has taken a family of virgins four years of afternoons to stitch, how to understand time?

The great luxury now, as it was not then, in the days of the flowered cushion, is to have other people to carry out what one could oneself be doing. That is supposed to free time in order for one to do what one does best. I was popularly, that is among our acquaintance, supposed to do thinking best, but it is not an easily evidence accomplishment. I had worked at a series of ill-paid though rewarding jobs with publishers, occasionally jazzed up by bouts on the boards and even, sometimes, if there was nothing else, modelling.

But now, freed from cooking by the cook, from cleaning by the cleaners, from John by Margaret, I was not carefree, nor was I full of thoughts.

I dared not sit still, for fear of being caught in apparent idleness, for which the only excuse might have been beauty or a decent literary output. Mine had been a glamour of animation which stillness had dulled.

Our house and garden were none the less a credit to those they kept employed. I liked to consider them, laid out and labelled, perspective absent and detail disproportionate as in a seventeenth-century estate map. Daily I added detail to this map as I oversaw the establishment of an asparagus bed or the installation of a machine to make hard water soft. As the great houses remind one of a city state, so ours reminded me of a hive, full of business tending to the making of sweetness and its storage. It is true that I did not feel myself the queen bee, but I knew that this would come with time and patience and practice. We had been married only five years.

The days passed and the nights lengthened. I was happy, my husband was happy, and we were happy with Margaret, who kept John happy.

Sometimes I thought the happiness was the better for not thinking. When I did try to think, I too often encountered my own objections to our way of life, as though I were a doctor who carries the disease he is attempting to cure.

It was simple not to think, easier each day.

I lived by instinct and its control, like a properly tended plant, and John was my flower and fruit.

As was natural, orderly, provident, I found out after one of the first very good shooting days on our land, with towering birds and a sporting wind, that I was pregnant.

The shooting cards were sent out to the guns. My husband kept his own. Our cards were pictorial, with each column for the various game shot headed by a reduced Bewick engraving of that creature, in life. One column was for miscellaneous beasts, shot not by design. In this column, my husband wrote "baby."

"If it's a girl, it'll be a left and a right all right," he said.

He could be very funny.

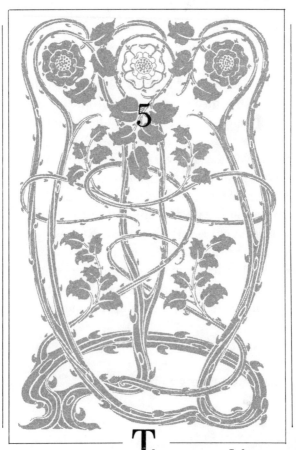

5

That autumn John started school. He learnt about shame and comparison, and a certain amount about short words. At school he met children he already knew and some new children. In the morning they made marks on soft sheets of col-

oured paper which they brought home after a story
and a rest. There was a sandpit at the school and a
roll of oil-cloth for handwork-fallout. There was a
frieze showing the happier events in the life of
Christ, and there was a list of names with stars
against them. John seemed to come between decent
brandy and a country-house hotel for conduct and
was about mid-octane petrol academically.

He made school jokes at home and said "Present"
when one called his name. He was, though, endear-
ingly absent, giving perfect attention only to what
interested him perfectly.

Margaret drove him to school. At the school she
met other nannies and after school they would sometimes go to a tea-shop for coffee and cakes. John
would be given glossy crackleware buns which he
could not finish. I would find the square sugar crys-
tals in the corners of his pockets. Her pleasures left
their sugary dust.

I was glad Margaret had made friends. In the evening she might meet the other nannies and they
would see a film or go out to eat. Those nannies who
were her particular friends tended to be those whose
employers were our particular friends.

The children got on well, only ever divided, and
that briefly, over possessions.

When other children came to see John, to play
with his toys or in his birthday-garden, the nannies

31

talked among themselves. They required music all day; the nursery radio played, unlistened to but never unheard, murmurous and inoffensive. John learnt words from the radio; he knew chart positions and dated words of soft hip slang. He described things as "fab" and "really over the top." On Margaret's day off there was no radio until my husband came home and listened to the shipping forecast. John loved this; he sat, quite silent, with his father, a careworn expression on his uncreasable brow. He also admired newspapers for their evident importance in the world where things were heavier to bear and trousers and silences were long.

Like many children's, John's first interjection had been "Oh dear." It is what first children hear that parents replace more forceful oaths with, a soft oath, a nursery lament, and from this they learn that life is a dangerous business, though we tell them before they sleep that elephants use lifts and rabbits wear blue coats with brass buttons.

Naturally, the nannies gossiped. I and my friends knew this because some of these friends gossiped with their nannies. It was cosy talk, scandal with milk, of babies, fiancés, naughtiness. Perks were compared, skiing holidays, access to video recorders, horses, time off. Wages, of course, and clothes, which were swapped for special parties. The main topic, however, seemed to be weight.

It did not seem to be the case that a nanny was a necessarily maternal woman. Margaret said that she and her nanny-friends (she described them thus, like nanny-goats) all agreed that they would not care to have children unless they had a nanny. Some of these young women were, like Margaret, saving to be married, others "did not like" the idea of marriage. Two had even been told, according to Margaret, that they could not have children. I thought this sad and possibly dangerous, but she assured me that they felt no more intensely towards the children in their care than the fertile nannies felt. How she knew this, I could not imagine. "Fertile" was her term, rhyming with "myrtle."

Not that the point of life is reproduction, only its end; but has not a nanny chosen, at any rate temporarily, children as the point of her life?

I had often thought that most professionals did not in fact care for what their parish, or patients, or clients, or material for these things' own sake, but for the return they brought. What possible return could these ordinary, if fortunate, children offer?

Whether or not Margaret and her friends were maternal, they were intensely engaged in struggling with what are considered motherly figures.

I had been right about Margaret when I deduced that she frequently changed shape. Food was of great importance to her, as adversary and as preoccupation. At the moment she was winning her struggle with it. When John ate, she did not, so it was by authority rather than example that she showed him how and what to eat. He was a good eater, with a distaste for puddings.

Margaret loved sweet things and her shopping bags were full of those strange foods made for consumers addicted to bulk and sweetness but desirous of no nourishment. She bought those strange costly foods whose colours are of an unconvincing brightness. She drank chocolate milk so thick it resembled a bodily secretion, cheesecake which sighed to the knife. At the end of each day she calculated the value in calories of all she had eaten. The refrigerator in the nursery kitchen was full of bright drinks in clear vessels like aqualungs, and bread the colour of snow. For butter she had grease which reeked faintly of town water and her jam contained neither fruit nor sugar but was red as ric rac. She did not seem to be aware that a lettuce and an omelette made from our own eggs would taste better and do her less harm than these weightless hefty meals of cloud and promise. In brown bags, John's food had its own place in the refrigerator, unseductive and plain.

Our farm produced meat, the garden vegetables, we had milk and eggs and the cook made bread. I wondered sometimes whether these things were too physical for Margaret to bear.

In my pregnancy, I grew fatter at the waist and continued to eat, as I always had, fresh, clean food, pickled and salted to an alerting brackishness.

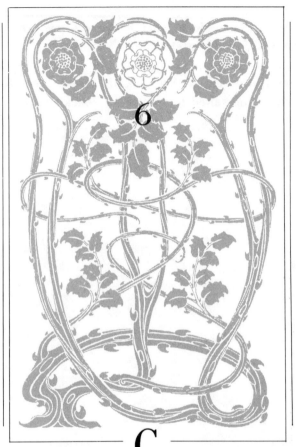

Christmas consolidated the happiness in the house. I stopped worrying about our felicity and settled to getting and spending.

We had two Christmas trees that year, one for ourselves and one for John and Margaret. He had decorated their tree with baubles and tinsel, which Margaret had chosen. Their tree was gayer than our own. They had spent a morning in the local town choosing frosty globes enclosing Bambis, and clip-on birds with smooth glass-fibre brushes for tails. She had painted a crib-set and given the eaves of the stable glitterdust for snow. The manger had a nicely sewn duvet of straw-coloured cloth, the size of a pictorial rather than simply monarchist stamp.

"I'm baby-minded," said Margaret, placing the infant Jesus.

She was to spend Christmas at her home.

"We shall all miss you," I said, as we handed over our presents the evening before Christmas Eve. She had done more than she need to prepare things for us and now driving off to help her parents with their celebrations. It was a strenuous time for her but she loved it. She had left a list for me, of outstanding preparations which could not be done too far in advance.

After we had said goodbye, John with kisses and my husband and I with boxed dainties and loud voices, I took out the list, which was written on her now-familiar paper. She dotted her *i*'s with circles like birds' eyes.

"I wouldn't lose her for all the world," said my husband, and he stretched and looked as self-satisfied as a painted paterfamilias.

I told him this. He was pleased and announced, "I'm looking forward to this Christmas more than to any other so far."

I agreed.

I took Margaret's list upstairs, where I went to turn off the tiny lights on John's small tree, now he was asleep. The sense of suspended sweetness in the new dark was like covering a songbird with its dark night-time cloth.

The list read:

24th Dec. Remember to rest for baby. Feet up. Cook off. 8 pm, peel potatoes and put under water, Brussels peeled and x'd? 10 pm, Johnny's stocking in my second drawer down. 11 pm, bird in slow oven of Aga. 12 pm, midnight mass. Say a prayer for Margaret!!

25th Dec. Bird in hot oven (did you take it out after mass?) at 10 am 11 am, church. J's British warm airing in boiler room, shoes, etc. ready. Collection in glove. 1 pm, eat a good dinner. No bread sauce. Onion bad for baby—and Mummy. 3 pm, John's and my gift to you in nursery kitchen pan cupboard. 4 pm, no more than two (2) mince pies for J. No brandy butter. Custard ready in fridge. Does not eat skin. 6 pm, drinks tray for villagers ready, except ice.

26th Dec., "Boxing Day." M. back. PHEW!

At the bottom, with the two ducks and their duckling, she had drawn a turkey, recognisable by his clerical wattles, uncooked, alive, raising his right drumstick in an avian—and presumably cannibalistic—grace.

I could not imagine what we would do without her.

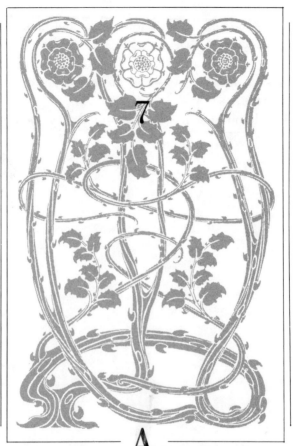

7

Asked about her own Christmas with her family, Margaret gave little away. It was as though her own home life did not enter the third dimension. She did not speak of her parents in the round. She appeared to have no childhood memories. When she released details, they were flat and lifeless as details from an instruction leaflet. It was as though she described self-assembly furniture. None the less, she wrote frequently to her family and to her boyfriend. She left her letters with mine, for the postman to pick up. My letters were to old friends, when they did not contain cheques.

I had also taken to writing enthusiastic letters to people I had admired on the television or had heard on the radio. I agreed with or differed so acutely from people I'd never heard of that I had to write to them. I was sheepish if they replied; by then I had generally forgotten them.

At New Year we had a large party for tenants and employees. Such occasions are intended for the continued good relations between the hosts and their guests in the dealings the coming year must bring. Their aim is not solely pleasure. Our New Year party was our office party, but we and our guests lived on and from the office, the land, and for its cultivation, disposal, allotment, finance, maintenance and that of the beasts, people and wild things living on it.

We engaged electricians to fill the garden with lights. We locked small treasures in the safe. John was interested in the safe, with its tubular oily bars and spinning combination disc.

"Twenty children a year die in disused refrigerators on tips, and they don't even lock," said Marga-

41

ret. She had stopped spelling out words she considered unsuitable, since by now John could coarsely spell.

"I could live nice in here," he said. For him, the safe was indeed the size of a house. "There are all stuff for eating."

"For eating off. Or with. Not for eating," I said. "Not for feeding off."

"We don't say feed, we say food," said my son and his nanny, like an old couple doing a turn. The cream, silky hair grew like a star on John's crown. The underhair was growing in grey-gold, the no-colour of wheat after the harvest and its hot moon. Margaret's soft hair was dun; over one temple a bright comb showed its teeth. She smiled.

"Do please bring your young man," my husband said to her. "We'll be all sorts, most informal."

"Will you bring him?" I asked later, at nursery tea. I would not by now have minded a more close relationship.

"Who?"

I realised I knew no name for him. I could not have been referring to anyone but her fiancé, but Margaret required clarity.

"Your beau." She must read that sort of romance.

She gave no reply; I might have been talking millinery. I saw clearly my own tendency to wrap up and enfold meaning, her own laudable cleanliness of mind, where all was what it seemed.

"Your boyfriend. The person you hope to marry."

She composed her face, retrieving its features from the throes of surprise admirably quickly.

"It's very difficult; the animals he works with are very demanding."

"No more demanding than John, surely?" I was making a joke.

She did not appear to enjoy the suggestion that she worked with animals.

"Johnny's a real little person," she said, in a voice made for church.

"Yes. A card," I replied, wondering why we denigrate what we love best. Knowing it was to keep off the gods' covetous eyes.

I asked what she intended wearing.

"Oh, that doesn't matter," she replied, smiling with her cheeks. "What are you wearing, we all want to know? There's talk of nothing but." We were back in the safe world of romance, hierarchy, display, garmentry.

I was getting bigger and could be comfortable in only two of my party dresses. I had hardly changed size while pregnant with John. Unprepared to find myself so swollen in this second pregnancy, I showed Margaret the two frocks, pulled out from the fallow silks, discarded *peaux d'oranges* and ashes of *faille* roses in my dressing-room.

It was to be either a wide black tent with a suggestion of jet at the shoulders, or a violet sheath with much orange lashing. Margaret liked the purple, and that decided me, as she was not loose with praise.

"You can carry it," she said, and encouraged me to put it on to show her and John.

I made up my face as it would be at our party, very pale, with an orange mouth and mauve eyelids. I tied a turban in my hair and tucked into its front a piece of jewellery the size of a fried egg, with two rashers of *pavé* rubies. My feet remained slim, so I put them into satin shoes with heels like knives.

"Fat wicked queen," said John.

"Pretty Mummy," said Margaret, her mouth neat and smacking as though at a soft centre.

Was school bad for my son?

The bump at my front looked like a corm. John appeared not to notice it. Margaret said he would not connect it with the baby she had told him was coming (she had explained that the news, from me, might make him jealous). I could see that it would be complicated to relate the bump and the baby in his mind without unnecessary information.

The day before the party, snow had fallen. The house in its park looked just snowy enough, as though figured in the recollection of a sweltering ex-patriate. We lived in a balmy part of England, much sung in war, always photogenic, conjured at times when memory and sentiment made of wives and hearths and smoothly looping rivers something desirable in their predictability. Our valley held no scrub and no untended woodland. It was impossible, as it is not in the north, to imagine wolves. If they had been there, they would have been as sleek and tame and good with children as the supreme vulpine champion of Assisi.

The house was terribly hot and full of noise. There was a smell of flowers and food, both meaty. People I did not know moved about with cables, drugget and keys. The policemen in their chesty dinner jackets arrived first, showing an area of shirt the shape and size of an unshriven sole.

By six o'clock, the policemen had stopped refusing drinks.

John went to bed at seven, very docile. I was not yet dressed for the party.

It was to begin at ten o'clock, and before that we had a few of our own friends to dine. I kissed John, bending over at the waist where my jeans could no longer fasten and were tied with an old tie of my husband's. My jersey was of that oily wool which cannot be washed in water, only with ash. Upon my face was a clay mask, dry as a grass court's lines.

"Mad witch," said John, touching my lips with his hand to make sure they were not chalky before kissing me.

"John Solomon, you solemn man." It was an old joke, and had always worked before. John's second name was his father's first. Sometimes, to myself, I called him Sol. His father, in his wisdom, ruled out any such abbreviation for himself. But the shortness of children does not make them less whole. We kissed, more in the air than on the lips, and I watched him roost into his pillow, insert his shining thumb, and fall down suddenly beneath the horizon of sleep.

Just before I dressed, Margaret came to me.

"He's unable to come," she said, clearly referring to her fiancé. "It's a last-minute emergency. No one else has the expertise. He's a responsible job to do."

I had missed the telephone's shrill in the bustle.

"I've put on John's alarm," she said, "as the house will be noisier than usual. We're all going to listen for him." She meant everyone who worked in the house.

I first saw her pretty black dress when I was going down the main staircase. At a certain turn, the door of John's room was visible.

She was wearing shoes with high heels and seemed to be slimmer. Her hair was not frizzy, but soft. It contained colours. At her neck it waved where before there had been stubble.

A soft bar of light from John's room cut the corner of the dark corridor, before she closed the door and turned on the landing light.

I smelled her scent. I had almost come to like it.

"Goodnight, pretty Margaret," said the awakened voice of my son, the words audible on the alarm, though distorted by amplification.

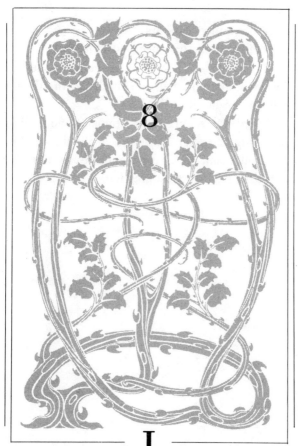

8

In winter, a marquee full
of dancers is a romantic thing, frivolous as a stall at
an ice fair. In each corner were tied bouncing
bunches of balloons, filled with a gas lighter than air.
They were red like redcurrants, thin scarlet stretched

with brightness. They stirred as the dancers moved, with a slow seething motion as though agglutinated in a medium of sugar sweetness.

A group of big men used to machines for cutting through wood and earth stood in one corner, drinking. They were not yet drunk enough to dance. The wives sat in another corner, sipping sweet mixture. Among them was Margaret. She was more smartly dressed than most of them, and she held, but did not drink from, a champagne glass. She resembled a woman in a television advertisement for chocolate mints, who had fallen among women advertising something homelier, washing powder, or discounted carpeting. I felt sorry for her, without her fiancé. No doubt she had bought the black dress for him. He must be curious about her job, concerned to know whether where she worked was pleasant, her employers fair, her wages given for a reasonably restricted amount of work.

"We must invite Margaret's fiancé some time," I said to my husband.

"Whatever for?" he replied. "Does he need a job?" He was off, elegant and menacingly jovial among his dependants in his festival clothes of white and black.

Men slapped his back and used his Christian name and our own friends talked to each other and not to us in order to leave us free to mix, to be perceived

not sticking to our own kind. I saw him move towards where the wives sat.

"Come the revolution," he would say, "I'll be a
butler, no problem. I love to fetch funny drinks."

I saw him smiling, fetching little glasses of gold
and orange and milk colours. Later, he would tell me
of the most outlandish concoctions. "And the awful
thing is, they call them names now, so I'm meant to
know the constituent parts of a Snow Goose or an
Open Bottom Drawer or whatever. Omo, lemonade
and Cointreau, or some such."

He was standing, fetching, stopping, never sitting.
It was a tradition at these parties that he should wait
upon those who waited, every other night, upon him.

To each wife, as he gave her her drink, he addressed some words. These women had almost all
known him since he had been a boy, but now he was
not only bigger than they were but looked as though
he came from an altogether larger race, meat-fed and
clothed in confidence. Down the sides of his trousers
ran a hardly shiny silk ribbon and his feet were slip-
pered in black velvet. Black satin faced his jacket.
The many surfaces of black about him made him rich
and solemn among the little women in pale dresses.
Many of them wore cardigans, like children at a
party, angora or snowy Orlon, showing the creases
where they had come from the packet.

"Very nice," they said to me when I went over.

"Very nice to see there's a new addition on the way. And how is John?"

And I could ask them about their children and grand-children, many of whom were at the party. It was easy, being a woman, with the democratic matter of children to discuss. I was quite happy there for a time, but felt I must move on, speak to everyone. As it was her first of these parties, I must see that Margaret was all right.

She was sitting with her back to me, her black bag set on the red-clothed table, facing one of the corners with its floating cluster of red balloons. I had to move sideways between the tables, though my height kept the bump of my belly above the backs of the little golden chairs, which appeared to be constructed of small gold femurs.

She was speaking to one of the gamekeepers. Her champagne glass remained an untouched accessory.

"He just works with animals," she was saying to him. The keeper was looking at her as though he wished he could describe his own job in some way which omitted all mention of animals. She was looking very pretty. Her eyes were bright, her nails pink, her femininity cocked.

"Hello, Robert," I said. "Happy New Year, nearly."

"I hope so," he said. "It could be very happy." He was known to "see to" the wife of one of the cow

51

men, but he needed a wife of his own. His eyelashes reached his eyebrows and the down on his cheeks was thick; his chest escaped his shirt. He looked at Margaret, who looked at her own hands. She was not wearing her engagement ring this evening, perhaps in pique at her fiancé's absence.

She took out a handkerchief from her bag, kissed it, leaving a pink mouth-shape on the cotton, and returned it to the bag. Had she suddenly felt the weight of all that pink frosting? My husband joined us briefly, standing behind Margaret's chair. The black jersey of her dress was seemly beneath his own swart radiance. I was glad she was having a nice time.

"Look, Robert," he addressed the keeper. "She's a nice girl to take out for an evening. Sober and cheap. You haven't touched a drop, Margaret. It's perfectly good, you know. The real thing."

"It's very nice," she said. "Pleasant." She took a sip, leaving, mysteriously, another pink mouth-mark on the rim of the glass.

"Nothing could induce me to touch strong drink," she had said to me. Evidently she had not meant "no one."

My husband looked relieved, Robert hot and help-less. He gazed into his own glass, which contained nothing.

"Let me see you right, Robert," said my husband. "What's it to be? Black and tan?"

Robert's glass was a tall straight flute, on a stem.

At midnight we released the balloons from the tethered bunches where they struggled for free air. They floated up to the roof of the marquee, bobbing against its inner membrane, striving to reach its highest points. Their ribbons hung down straight as stems from the light jostling red fruits.

Optimistic, frail and ignorant of the future, we sang. You might have thought we were all workers in the established legal firm Auld, Laing & Syne.

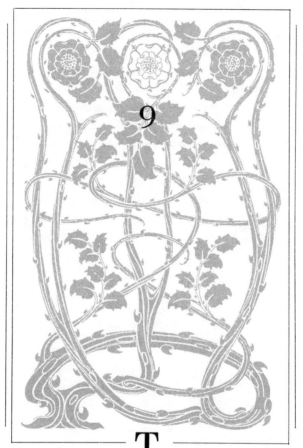

9

The next morning, the bal-
loons were for John. He and Margaret and my husband and I, wrapped against the snow, collected
them in the cold marquee. We three adults climbed
ladders to catch the tails of the balloons, and passed

these wilful bouquets down to John. He was simmering with pleasure. Margaret was wearing a hat which said, around its woolly brim, "Nanny Knows Best." My husband had found it for her Christmas present.

A group of chairs to which John, helped by Margaret, had tied towering bunches of balloons, began, at one point, to dance, on their bony gilt points.

When we were all tired, and the last balloon was tamed, we ate lunch in the marquee, its lining stirred by the snowy wind, which had made us hungry. The light lining, passing against the heavy canvas which supported and protected it, made again and again the sigh of elegance assaulted by cold, the gentle, vain susurration of a consumptive's ghost.

Margaret removed her hat. My husband forced it on to one balloon, which seemed at once to become the most rebellious and flighty of them all. John laughed, excited to bouncing. He was impressed by all these new pleasures.

"I am five now," he said, "because it is a New Year."

"You'll die young if you travel that fast," said Margaret.

We were sitting at the only table without its ballast of balloons. The balloons creaked and bumped together. The noise was that of a boat moored in fog, the soft bump and lift and complaining of the fenders and the ordinary yet exaggerated sounds of invisible movement.

"This food really is fabulous," said Margaret, though it was only flaccid sweet ham and oozing salads.

John was interested in the strains made by my beetroot.

"Look at the beetroot carefully and you'll see how old it is by the number of rings it has," said his father.

"Margaret sometimes has one ring," said John.

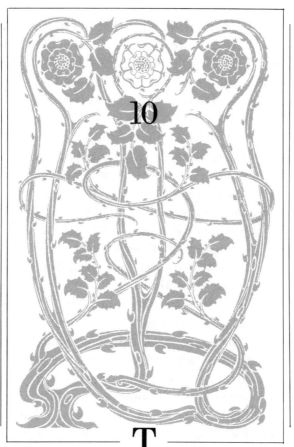

10

The spring came, unassumingly, as though perhaps it had not been invited. Through their snoods, like garlic-paper, nipped the milk teeth of snowdrops. The cellar smelt more of bulb fibre and less of gun oil. Our social life, which all winter had taken place between freezing days outside and terrifying drives home, began to calm down. We were less often drunk over ice, driving at speed with hot clear heads full of spirits and deaf from gunfire. I began to feel congruent with the year, holding new life.

Margaret purchased a new jumper. It celebrated the springtime. Although it was made of the wool of lambs, it showed the floral rather than the animal attractions of the season. About her grew tall woollen daffodils, their trumpets little yellow finger stalls, in bas-relief from her curving breast. John loved the jumper; he fingered the trumpets with relish.

"There was a cardy with foxgloves, but it didn't look very nice," said Margaret.

"How so?" asked John, an expression he had from me, so I liked him to use it.

"Never you mind," said Margaret, rolling her eyes at me in alliance, adult female knowledge protecting the child from those flowering purple towers in our minds. I found it hard to imagine spending my professional life knitting priapic mauve cosies, but were my bits of work any more necessary than that? Nor could anyone be said to be kept warm by them.

Inside our house women worked; in the garden men were employed. There were two women who cleaned, and one who cooked; there was Margaret and there was me. No two of us were equal, though I felt that it was not I who established the hierarchy. There was me, useless but essential, with the others below, each at her allotted, or, it may have been, chosen, level. The women who cooked rarely did so for Margaret, though sometimes there was a bartering of delicacies, if the adults were eating something to John or Margaret's taste. He loved savouries and would beg for cheese. Margaret discouraged this, so he learnt to approach the big kitchen when she was busy. He liked the peelings of winter vegetables, and might sit beside Lizzie as she made stew; he did not eat them, but he dropped them from a height on to the chapped wooden table to see what letters they made when they landed; *j* came often, and *s*, and *m*, for "Margaret"; and for "Mummy." The clean smell of shucked roots and the sweetness of cooking parsnips clung to his hair, so Margaret would find him out.

"Eating piggy food again, young sir?" she would ask, and sweep him off for a hairwash. With the side of her knife, Lizzie would push the squared roots she had been saving for John into the deep pan she clipped to the table with one hip. She was sensible and knew children, having had several. She was not discontented with repetition, but comforted by it, so that her cooking and her conversation had a soothing constancy. She was free of any urban compulsion to entertain, so she was always interesting; her hair was long and rosy grey, and she read books in one hand as she stirred with the other. It used to be on her days off that I composed my tart feasts. Lizzie seemed to like Margaret. I had never heard her discuss people, unless through the foods they favoured. I hoped that she did not realise my tastes.

Her husband worked in the garden; they conspired to grow and to cook really enormous leeks, like organ pipes, from one trunk of which she could wring vichyssoise for ten. Sliced across, these monsters resembled white short-playing records. This seemed to be Lizzie and Basil's only vagary.

Then there were Edie and Bet. Edie's mother and father had worked in this kind of household, already fairly anachronistic, when, in their late middle age, Edie was born. She was an old-fashioned girl, a loved late child, quiet and sober. She was in her thirties, pretty, unpainted and stern; she had a straight back and wore straightforward clothes, like those of a middle-class child in the 1950s. Sometimes she laughed until she cried. If anyone exaggerated, including me, she said something to deprecate the needless inflation. She looked like someone who might have a singular, solitary talent, marquetry or the violin. Her husband was a research biologist. Her privacy was complete.

Bet in private was unimaginable; she was entirely public. Her hair was red, her mouth was red and often her eyes were too. Occasionally one of them was black and yellow. She was a tub with tiny hands and feet; she always wore high heels. She crashed things about as though she were working in a hospital. She made rude jokes, and indented regularly for a pay rise, to keep up, as she explained, with her friend who worked at the meat-packing depot.

"Hi," she would say, "it's the shop steward." And she would come into my morning-room with a cup of coffee for me and a list of requests. Her sons were always in trouble, stealing or playing truant, and her husband lost work intermittently when he was "badly." She loved pretty things and was violently maternal. "Oh, John," she shouted, "oh, look at you. I could eat you on toast." She kissed him wetly on his neck and played with his striped hair. From most people he flinched, but he loved Bet. She bought him presents she could not afford, and often asked to take him home with her. To John too this was an unspeakably glamorous prospect. She swore terribly but never acknowledged this with apology, so the bad words were not salient. Bet had done everything: she had wed a bigamist, she had been to Canvey Island every summer all her life. Both her natural parents were dead, but had left relicts—Bet's stepparents— who lived with her and her husband and their boys. Bet had romantic plans for her stepmother and stepfather. Her husband bred fancy guinea pigs with whorls in their fur; sometimes she brought one for John to look at, in a box, in the back of her car; the box had come as a rule from the supermarket, after dark, containing slightly sub-standard crisps, or imperfect pizzas. Bet knew where to get seconds of the already most inedible foods; her best connection in this way was the friend who got her unlabelled cans. "Could be giblets, could be niblets, they're not fussy but I must say I would not eat those dirty pheasants if I was paid. I seen what they eat."

Our own pheasants were hand-reared by Robert and his helper and ate pheasant food and then, in the brief glorious autumn of sex and showing off, the berries and worms growing and thriving upon our land. Their crops, when they were drawn, were often fat with soft good grain, grown to perfection under the best supervision, the grain which fed the people. What could she mean?

I was dead-heading the more undimmable hybrid roses, quite pleased to be in at the extinction of their brightness, when Bet came out to me. Something must be worrying her for she did not like the out-of-doors; it spoiled her heels, she said, and gave her a wicked appetite. During the short season of soft fruit, she stopped wearing her tripping heels and wore white plimsolls which were pink by its end.

"How d'you get them white for next year?" Edie would ask.

"Boil them for gym-shoe jam, Ede, what'd you do?"

"Wear boots."

Today Bet had come in her high red pumps, down the garden to the longest border. There had been no frost for days and the sun was encouraging the garden to rashness. Tiptoeing so as not to sink into the paths, she recalled someone afraid to wake a sleeper.

I called to her, "Go on the grass, in your bare feet," but she grimaced and continued her dainty progress. These scarlet roses were grotesque in age; they had bletted like fat tan onions. They plopped on to the canvas donkey I had put down at the border's edge.

"Damp grass on my bare feet drives me to feel I'll vomit," said Bet. "The worst of all being seaside turf, making the reason why I will not stand picnics. But I'll stand on this bit of cloth if I may, so's I don't end up in Australia, even if in my best shoes."

"Might be nice in Australia, at the moment. All that sun." I was rocking my clippers about a tough sucker. "Still," and I clipped through it, "I don't much like the idea of turkey under the sun, do you? Or do you?"

"You may and you may not like it, but I'm here to say it." Bet was a short woman and she was squint-

ing up at my leafy head. I tried to coil up the long
thorny sucker, could not, and chopped it in four. Its
lowest thorns were hooks of grey, the fresh ones a
translucent scarlet in the sun. I laid down these rosy
scourges on the earth.

"Yes?"

"I can't talk to a tree." I came out of the border
altogether; at least Bet let me know exactly where I
stood.

"With my boys, I don't always listen, but I've always got ears to hear."

"Something's happened to one of the boys?"

"It's not one of my boys, it's your one boy; it's
only a small thing, but I don't like it. Tell me to mind
my pros and cons if you like. I don't want to worry
you, or anything." She was suppressing her natural
gossip's instinct to spin out a small mystery; that was
a mark of her affection for John.

"What is it, Bet?" I was not badly concerned, because I trusted her to show upset in proportion to
what had caused it. "Have you heard him saying
something bad, swearing or something?"

"As if I'd be the one to fuss about that. No; it's
that Margaret. She's all so ever so nice, I know, but
she can't listen out for him properly."

I didn't want to hear petty tale-telling; I had over-
estimated Bet.

"What do you mean?"

"She takes him for a walk, sometimes even in the car, and she has him playing with her, but she can't hear him. She has her soundtracks on the whole time."

"Soundtracks?" I thought of a soundtrack for John, full of cooing and yelling and practice-sentences and the disappearing lisp.

"Small earphones with loud music in. A sort of personal record-player. Kind of thing."

"Oh, those things. But I didn't know Margaret had one of those. After all, she listens to the radio all day."

"Probably doesn't know if it's off or on. Like those people with no nerves, the ones in Russia. They couldn't tell you if their appendix has burst, let alone if some little kid had hurt itself."

"But why should he hurt himself? Isn't Margaret always with him?"

"In a manner of speaking. But you can't really chat to someone in one of those outfits; I should know that. My boys sleep in them. I'd as soon have had a blind dog look after my boys as a girl in all those wires."

"Hold on, Bet, I've not even seen her doing it."

"Of course you've not." She gave a meaning look. "And is it that bad anyway?"

Deprived of her pellet of malice, Bet seemed disappointed. She sighed hard, and rolled her right thumb around and around the nail of her right index finger, looking down at her pointed red shoes among the thorns and used roses. She sighed again, theatrically, and muttered. What I heard was ". . . the heart doesn't grieve after."

These spats were to be expected in a house full of women.

I decided that I would speak to my husband if I saw an opportunity.

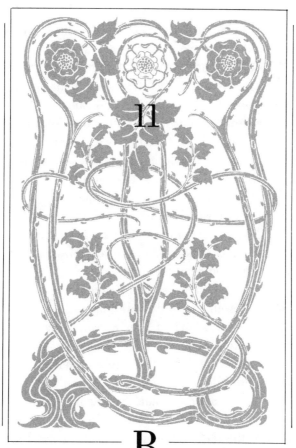

11

Bet and Edie arrived in
the morning, just as John left for school. After
school, too, he crossed with them, arriving as they
left. He was becoming less womaned, losing these
first sweethearts with whom he had flirted. That

home-bound infant world, in which the broom cupboard and the kitchen are gynaecea, and the smells
of Windolene and Brasso as feminine as attar, was
shrinking. Bet and Edie, from being his intimates,
were becoming to him people who came to clean the
house, a thing he saw his parents not doing. To Margaret, I do not think that they were ever more than
cleaners, though she did take a break with them halfway through the morning. They drank tea or coffee
and ate what Lizzie called "ferocious quantities" of
cakes, winged with icing-soldered sponge, or sand-
wiched with glistening mocha. Margaret drank
skimmed-milk milkshakes and valueless ducats of
impacted puffed rice.

There is a fatuous state in pregnancy when you
know all is well, not only with yourself but with the
world. You know that a species which has evolved
this miraculous system of reproducing itself, the
natty idea of containing the future empursed within,
cannot allow destruction to obtain, will not short-
change us. You know that, by placing your gravid
body between the light of ugly fact and the unde-
fended of the race, you can cut out the glare. I knew,
because I had been pregnant before, that it is a fleet-
ing sense of beneficient glowing power, preceding almost invariably a certainty that all shadows are black
and all breaths our last, a time during which tears—
selfish tears of easy altruism—are never far away,

and the newspapers are sopping before their finer print is even begun. I was at the first stage, though, when Bet brought a box into my bedroom, where I stood, squiffy with optimism, showering benevolence upon the bare trees through my window, and on the birds within them—those organised pheasants and the less well-bred members of the parliament of fowls. My turbine of confidence and virtuous energy was capable of anything. I could have illuminated a city with the touch of my finger. I was equal to anything; after all, what could, in this good world, harm me, who contained the point of it all? I could see clearly that, since there was no argument for destruction, there would be no destruction. This dangerous drunken clarity is the closest I have been to escaping the omnipresence of the end. Painting and music remind me, the greater they are, the more of death.

I was hailing the broad day when Bet came in with her box.

"I've got a guinea pig. It's for John. Seeing as my husband breeds them for show, this one won't do. It was a guinea pig, you see."

"Was?"

"It is a guinea pig, but it was a guinea pig. In a sense. I mean, we were trying something. A bit different."

A mutant. Swivelling off its balanced golden axis, my mind went to the beasts we cannot ignore, the footless shrikes and tubeless snakes, the eyeless cats of a poisoned nature, post-war fauna of our future.

A minute before, I had known all that would never be, and now the word—mutant—had discharged me from my oasis into a desert where war was inevitable and sin weighed as little as good. Pregnancy; is it by definition an hysterical state?

"Bet, is this guinea pig anything to do with me?"

"My husband says we can't show it and we wondered if John would like it."

Could I accept a possibly bald or tripod or varicose playmate for my lovely boy?

"It is kind of you, Betty, but . . ."

She ate the inside of her mouth. Lipstick bloodshot the slack skin around it. Her earrings, dependent from fatty lobes, appeared disposable, tatty.

". . . but let me see," I finished.

Its whorls were too vehement for the strict rules of the guinea pig fanciers, that was all. It was a fat cadpig with a square head like the heal of a snowboot. It was chinchilla-grey, with wet eyes and coiffed with frosty rosettes. Its hands looked intelligent, as though they might have known what to do with a cigarette.

"It's got a nice nature. Well, it sleeps all day. If you say the word, I'll get the husband and my sons to bring up its equipment."

Bar-bells, bookcase, Mouli?

"It needs a thorough combing, so I've got it this nice brush—a babe's brush, really. Basil's said he'll get a pen."

"A pen." In old-fashioned girls' stories, the helpless offspring of jungle creatures were always fed with a Waterman bulb. So the same was true of guinea pigs.

"You know, for it to run around in."

"Of course. Basil probably doesn't know his nibs."

Bet looked at me without concern. I was increasingly conscious that only I heard the lower layers of my own remarks. She smiled, and I was back on the planet euphoria, all refugees food to my egocentric charity. Let it rain guinea pigs.

"Bet, John will be so pleased. How can I thank you enough?"

"There'll come a time," said Bet.

She took the animal downstairs. I did not know its name or sex, but I was committed to it.

I continued the day's tasks, gluttonous of action and achievement, certain of immortality, carrying its pledge within me. I wrote letters, paid bills, made of my own desk and my husband's geometric altars to the rational mind, and was just believing in the perfectibility of all nature—about to eat the, in my eyes, freakishly beautiful boiled eggs Lizzie had made for

my lunch, cupped in unimprovable blue and white—
when Margaret came in.

I turned my dazzling smile upon her, *urbi et orbe.* I
could make all things right.

"Can I speak for a moment? It must be a moment,
as John's back in ten minutes." She counted her time
like her calories.

"Come in; sit down." I was delighted. Perhaps she
was about to unbend a little.

"Betty showed me the guinea pig, but it makes no
difference. I've told her time and again I won't have
animals. She's taken it away, of course. But mean-
while we shall not tell John."

I said nothing. She appeared to take this as mute
resistance.

"I really hate small things," she said.

In her energetically made vernal jersey she
seemed firmly planted in the room. My verve left me,
as though from a sprung leak. As I formed the sen-
tences with which to defy her, I began queasily to
feel that it was Bet and I, not she, who had been
sneaky. I heard the gulped slam of a car door and the
happy officious voice of my son, towards which Margaret—the pearl—turned and walked.

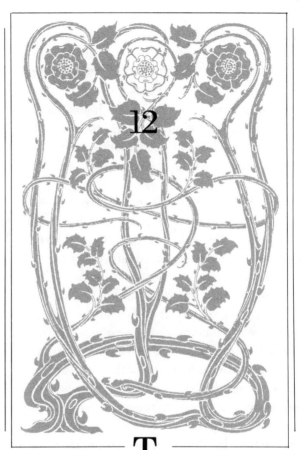

12

The pampering spring air
and easy days continued through March, and John,
who never knew about the pet he almost had, was
busy trying out different friends. He had a friend
with old knees who had only his parents to care for

him at home. I liked this child, though I was afraid of seeing in him virtues our way of life might preclude John from developing. He was a blithe boy, John's friend Ben, and he had a sensible exploitative attitude to the amenities of our house. Once he arrived with a satchel of mending; to his mother, who was dropping him off, he explained with some tact, "I've got my work in there," the image no doubt of his father.

Now the shooting season was over, the wives living round about were able to have lunch with each other again; the ease of segregation returned. This reversion to a less manned life was part of spring, welcome after the dark, rushed lunches of meat and neat spirits, with the guns talking from both barrels.

Today some of my friends and I were to meet at the house of Leonora, our closest neighbour. She was married to a man who had swarthy skin and blond hair, so he always looked healthy. He was as compact of energy as a battery; he had no languor. His energy seemed wisely invested. You could not mention something he had not done, and show he had done; yet he was modest. He invariably asked the right questions. The parts of his life, I felt, were all of a piece, in spite of their diversity. Yet he seemed to have time to read, and time for his wife.

My friends and their husbands were made for the sun and it sought them out. They were not fashioned for doubt or poverty or disappointment. The women wore gold and blue: golden chains and golden rings; blue and white clothes and blue and white precious stones. They did not paint much, and always smelt sweet. Each of their names ended, feminine to the last, with an *a*. At regular times, they went to different and far-flung parts of the blue and white and golden known world. The khaki areas of desert and armies were unvisited.

Like that china which, though unmatching, may be arranged together, always prettily—the blue bridges, blue pagodas, faint cerulean follies, pale azure branchlets, blowsy ultramarine galleons, all on differently white grounds—these girls (women was too biological a term) went happily together, and each also had other sets to which she belonged, all similar of aspect, yet each member individual. They did not displace time with worry or regret. They shared religion; they shared a masseuse. The same wall-eyed Cypriot sold them all heavy cold sheets hoared with lace.

I describe a chorus, yet each had her own tone. They were accomplished, even virtuoso, in some things, but, tactful, they did not overdevelop any trait. Their feet were narrow; their children beautiful. What they told was the truth. They wore flowers in summer, furs in winter. They were tough, too, beneath the freshness and softness. There was nowhere, no hinge or crack, for a blade to slip in. High-fired good china, perfect as an egg, and enclosing good, rich life.

Each had her nanny.

The eating part of lunch was swiftly over and we drank water. I took my lead from my friends, who never paid much attention to food for themselves, though they made sure their husbands had the best. We sat about Leonora's dining-room table. The door of the hexagonal room was a little ajar and through it came the singing yells of children. The nannies' voices did not carry.

"Close the door, Antonia, would you? Just a short break from the monkey-house, I think, don't you?" Leonora was pouring coffee into cups the colours of different fondants. In her place I might have worried about shutting out a fatal accident.

The room was full of that dazzling spring sunshine which makes you unreasonably pleased. A faint smell of warm cloth exuded from the green silk walls, mixing with the smells of coffee and blossom. A large bowl of viburnum filled the fireplace with lace.

"At least *we've* got zookeepers," said Antonia. She had five children, all of them light-hearted and intelligent and devoted to their mother, who now chocked her square face abruptly into her left hand, and waved her right, hailing a light for her cigarette. The ashtrays were like flat silver sombreros. Looking around at my slender, unpregnant friends, I felt as though I were barded with a suit of fat.

Victoria stretched in front of me, with a flaming knuckle, and the smell of smoke threaded among us. As she reached, her fringe caught and tossed away the sun. She had a sandy face with dark eyes and thin hands and legs like a boy, or the sort of fashion model who is chosen for her physical embodiment of intelligence; her voice was thorny. To drive, she wore glasses, whose rims were the peat-red of her hair.

"What if they turn out to be real horrors?" she asked. "I mean liars, or cruel."

"I wouldn't have it," replied Leonora.

"No choice," hooted Julia over the table, picking up a pebble of sugar and nipping it between her front teeth.

"Who're we talking about?" Clara was rifling in her basket and when she lifted her head her hair rocked back into place, smooth as a ball. Her eyes were sad at their outer edge, set into her head like two blue almonds of blue paisley. They were outlined with black. She began to sew, the looping movements of the needle less restful than the formal quietus of smoking.

"Who d'you think, Clara?"

"What do we always talk about?"

"Children."

"Try again. I mean, would the little angels ever lie or be unkind?"

"I meant nannies," said Leonora.

"I meant children," said Victoria, "but now we're on nannies let's stay there. It's not as though they weren't discussing us. I wonder whose husband is being turned into sausages right now."

"Something rather more solid, I bet," said Clara.

"Dawn tells me they snaffle the blue videos the men watch after shooting teas, and look at them after bath-time."

"She never told you herself."

"Not totally. Freddie saw a bit of one when he went down to her with a bad dream. He said she was looking at a telly programme about schoolteachers and naughty boys and I took it from there. Any luck it'll put him off and he can look after his poor old ma in her latter years."

"D'you remember that one who said she was the Red Hand of God? Some muddle there?"

"The holy rolling one with the sacred-text soap?"

"The very one."

"And the homesick one with the telephone calls to Ballachulish."

"I like those ones. It's the ones with men in the bed and moans of pleasure who make me feel tired."

"What about the one who was addicted to ringing ambulances? Had to go in the end when Viv fractured his skull and they wouldn't come out here. She'd a thing about the uniform."

"How would you feel, looking after someone else's kids, though? You might fancy a bit of company."

"And in the end they usually go and the children love us and forget them. It isn't such a great job. You can't get rid of your mum, short of murder. It's not like it was for nannies."

"Nannies aren't like they were. I wouldn't want to have a devoted nympho of ninety-two living in the north wing, listening to Hard Crack on the Walkman and thinking dope fudge was interesting."

"They go when they're unhappy, anyway."

"There must be something up with Dawn. She seems to've been happy with us for eight years."

"It's because you let each other be but you know what goes on, I guess."

"I don't draw the line very low, do you?"

They were all laughing by now, butting in. I didn't answer Victoria's question.

They were all fortunate in the girls they had to help them bring up their children. We all were.

"Stealing. I s'pose. Big stealing, not just wee extras on the side of bills."

"Stealing my husband."

"Going for people with knives."

"Blind drunkenness on the school run, maybe."

"Killing one or more of the children."

"Alienating the affections."

"What's that when it's at home?"

"It's never in a proper home," I said.

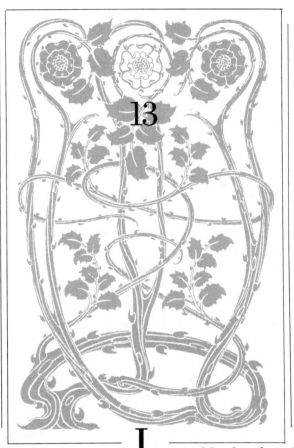

13

Late in March, when the game birds of the country concentrate on reproduction and revenge (chuckering asterisks of feather forcing fast cars to brake on bad corners, dying to teach their drivers a lesson), my husband was ready

to leave for a fortnight in London. Even before the
shooting had ended he was bored, so the sport of the
season was oysters, before the town's blossom came.

The wheat was drilled and the lambs born, the
fiscal year's end a fortnight off. I was too heavy and
too tired to join him. These bouts of man's business
and men's company transfused him. He would come
back important and happy, ready again for home.
John and Margaret, John and I, would go up to visit
him. He missed John terribly but always said London
was no place for the child. Besides, there was school,
and Easter was late that year, so we could spend it all
together.

I was pleased. Solomon would be safe and amused
in London. I was restive and uncomfortable at night,
sleepy by day, no companion for a man in spring-
time. Moreover, I was by now very large. It was as
though the baby was growing to enclose me, wrist for
wrist, ankle for ankle.

Once you are pregnant, you have an unbreakable
appointment to meet a stranger. I spent hours in a
state of mental submersion, just lying or sitting; my
eyes might as well have been shut. I was happiest
literally submerged weightless in a warm bath. Then
I felt my mind lift and play its light among the bland
rotund considerations of that time. Mostly I was living off a sustaining solipsism, contemplating for
hours tiny changes in my body, ribbons of silvery

stretched skin on my legs and arms, blue stars of exploded capillaries, little junks and caiques of white beneath my moony nails. I watched the plundering of my own body for minerals by the miner within. I wondered, indulgently, which part of myself I would find missing next. A sense of the self has never been my strongest suit: I deemed it no dishonour that I was being dismantled.

One night, I even dreamed a person of no gender came and took my teeth, with a special tool a bit like a dibber. There was no pain, but I knew I needed my teeth for something.

Unable to sleep after that dream, though as a rule my creamiest sleep was in the early morning, I went to see John. He was not asleep either, I could hear from the pigeon-sounds from his room. He was singing and talking. He had not yet become, as he did later in the day, some sort of vehicle.

"Good morning," he said, without looking up. "Tell me again about the scissor-man. Like last night."

"It's me, John." I particularly disliked the scissor-man, the bladed creature who jetés across a page in *Struwwelpeter,* and whose vocation it is to chop off the thumbs of children who suck them. I read it in German first, so perhaps I'm not being fair; maybe I inherited something of my father's antipathy. But even in the un-Gothick English script, I didn't like it.

The most unpleasant thing, to me, are the severed stumps where the thumbs have been, which spout blood like the roses of watering cans. But we didn't have a copy of the book in the house.

"Hello, Mummy. Did you suck your thumb when you were young?"

"Yes, and I've still got two thumbs. The scissor-man isn't true, you know."

"It is so."

"He is not."

"So."

"Not."

We began one of those padded tickling matches which end up on the floor. I was wrapped in my shrinking dressing-gown like a Sumo after a bout.

We were lying on the floor, out of breath. John said, "Pick on someone your own size. That's what Margaret said."

"Isn't Margaret bigger than you?" I asked with sleepy pedantry.

"She said it to the man."

"What man?" I was a bit confused. John knew the names of most of the people he saw.

But he heard my interest and didn't like the draught it let in from the grown-up world. Like his father, he had a way of cutting out when a subject had stopped being convenient. I resisted it sometimes, but that morning I thought he had as much right to be lazy, to have a time off thinking, as I had. When I had thoughts, I did not much like them.

Later, when I was dressed, I went up to the nursery to fetch John to say goodbye to his father.

"Margaret, are you very against the sucking of thumbs?" I was unnecessarily nervous, may even have spoonerised my question.

She looked up with surprise from John's nape, at which she was doing up some Fair Isle buttons that were cleft like toffee-coloured beetles, and replied, "It's nothing a spot of aloes can't cure." She enunciated very clearly and patiently.

"Aren't they awfully bitter?"

"They are known as bitter aloes."

"That's undeniable."

John raised his eyebrows at me. This adult gesture on his unlined face was funny, and he saw that I was doting on him. I felt quite warm with it. How could I ask questions about strange men, scissor-limbed or not, in front of him?

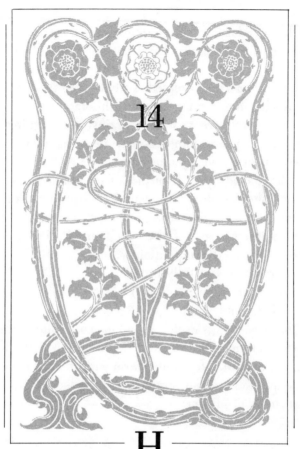

14

He wore his cars well, my husband. In the country they were green or nicely combat-muddied milk-white, of a square and accommodating cut. For town they were sharp and slim, though long enough for evening glamour. A car once bought loses its value; among the many ways we notionally lost money, this was one of the swiftest. One of the town cars was black and the other the hardly different blue which is darker than black. It is the blue of a king's greatcoat when he inspects his maritime forces, themselves a sea of merely navy blue.

Today he was driving himself, in the blue car. Having shut his papers in the boot, he allowed John in on his knee to say goodbye. It seemed strange, within that tank of pearly leather, tortoiseshell-walnut veneer and needled numbers, to see so much naked flesh, four unshelled limbs sticking out of shorts and a shirt, and a face without reserve, smiling beneath his father's face.

My husband lowered the window to allow me to look through air, not glass, at his son and himself. I stood away from the car so that I might bend, seeing as I did so my wide and layered reflection, like a pile of tyres, in the sleek side of the car. Thin as the line of red alcohol in an Arctic thermometer, the stripe down the side of the car sliced my inflated reflection at the belly.

"Look at Mummy," said my husband. "She's got a surprise for you, Johnboy. A secret surprise." He paused. "And I'll bring you back lots of surprises too."

"Boys or girls?" asked John, greedy but nervous.

"Cars, maybe, even," said his father.

I could see John thinking. His eyes went black and he flicked the silvery barrels of his sandals' buckles, which were between his father's blue-clothed knees. I thought I knew what he was thinking. He had connected my size with the baby to come, but he had just worked out that there might also be within me a train set, a fire engine, a build-it-yourself airport, with planes.

He put on a foolish voice. His father could be wooed with disingenuous words. I had seen him with the shady sapphire merchant, the mandrill-faced bullion-brokers with a line on Cayman postes restantes. John could be quite as effective.

"Is Mum having a sportscar then?" he asked, in the horrid clever voice of a punchlining comedian entertaining the mentally unadvantaged. This was a good voice for reaching my husband, who preferred his jokes signposted. But he had lost the thread, was thinking his way into Holland Park and down to our house.

"Mmmm?" he asked. It was an endearing noise, lazy. He had heard, but did not want to make the effort to think up a reply.

"No," came a voice from behind me. "No. And what's more you know no."

It was Margaret, come to say goodbye. She was removing her apron, a polythene-coated one, with a noise like a struggling fish. It was a large apron for a short person, but it had a lot to say. It related the calorific value of many basic foods; its one pocket, big enough to hold perhaps fifty thousand calories in potato form, said:

"But lovin' good
  Consumes dat food."

"Hop in, Margaret. Ever been in one of these?" said my husband.

She opened the back door for herself, as though that were the new part of the experience, and sat in the middle of the back, the least comfortable spot in that fast comfortable machine. Looking at her face, I understood suddenly the romance of cars. It was like watching a chicken getting into an orgone box. The car curved and returned. She emerged a phoenix.

"You're nice to please. Easy to please, too," said my husband, letting out the radiant bird.

We all three waved him off as he turned slowly along the front of the house. It was still too cold for the gravel to spit. Instead it crunched like rich cake and no dust rose to dull the low dense hedges of box that flexed like congers in the wake of the big car.

The question of John's strange man again occurred to me, but I couldn't see a way of bringing the subject up tactfully. Looking around, I could see nothing of which to make an apropos. Our house, the day, the flowers, it all appeared so feminine; how could I fracture it just because my son had invented a person whose only characteristic was that he was bigger than Margaret? Perhaps all children did it; something to do with challenging authority. I decided to wait until a clear opportunity arrived.

"John, you go upstairs. Margaret wants to talk to Mummy," said Margaret. She often spoke of herself in the third person, as though telling a story. It was comforting; it seemed the story's ending could only be happy, for the telling of it was so dull, a small narrative of journeys up and down stairs, of food taken in, of unrememberable acts.

He began to hurl up the back stairs, the banana-coloured crêpe of his shoes kissing the treads alternately, as he leaned his left side against the wall; he was torn between getting upstairs to play and staying downstairs with . . . Margaret, or me, or perhaps just the possibility of a biscuit.

Margaret led the way to my morning-room; it was as though she felt more able to talk in there, as if people might be listening elsewhere.

"It's nothing serious," she said. Certain denials declare their opposites; this was one of them. I felt the beat of panic, but asked, "What isn't serious?"

"I went to see the doctor yesterday. He gave me a piece of news."

"Our doctor?" She was registered with him, but had wished to keep her own doctor too.

"My doctor." She must have seen my puzzled look.

"I thought I'd better make it my doctor. You see, it's something John did."

"John? But he's a child."

"Oh, it's nothing. But I thought I'd better tell you in case anything happened."

So far I was not very worried. I did not think it possible that John had done anything very bad, and the mystification was beginning to irritate me.

"What on earth is it, Margaret? I can't bear the suspense."

She gave me a look of dignified injury.

"I am sorry; were you rough-housing?"

"No. I don't do that. But I am afraid he has blinded me in one eye."

"*Blinded* you, Margaret? You don't mean blinded, he can't have . . . ." I was aware of gabbling; I only wanted it not to be true. "When did it happen, where, no really, I mean how bad is it?"

I looked (my own two eyes a guilty weight in their sockets) hard at her eyes. They were surrounded with a powdery colour, sort of carrageen green. The irises were a clear hazel; the pupils identical unadapting black circles. Did one, the left one, look rather puffy? I was beginning to feel very sick.

Margaret stared back at me with a kind of weird, holy, stillness. I remember thinking, dazedly, that it couldn't be a joke, because she didn't have a sense of humour.

If someone says they are blind in one eye, one cannot very well disbelieve them. They are halfway to Gloucester; and in a great deal worse than a shower of rain. I felt bad for Margaret, and also frightened and defensive about my gentle son.

"It happened a couple of days ago; it could have happened to anybody."

"But it happened to you, for God's sake."

She looked very put out at the personal turn the conversation was taking. If she could have indicated her indisposition, like a Chinese lady, with a chopstick pointing to the relevant part of an ivory figurine, I felt she would have.

"Oh, I'm sure it'll get better; the doctor almost said so."

A fit of blindness, a passing blindness; was it possible?

"I must ring him. I want to know exactly. Oh, Margaret, how did it happen? It must be the most appalling shock."

I felt as though we had breached some biblical law of hospitality: do not blind your house guest or your servant. I thought of the charry stick poking Polyhemus's eye, a huge anemone.

Although the information was desperate, Margaret's attitude seemed so mild that I didn't know how to behave.

"I think I'll just be philosophical," she said. "I'd rather you didn't call my doctor until I've . . ."

I interrupted her. "You'll want to stop working right away, won't you?"

"If you don't mind, I will not. It's just a small thing."

I thought wildly of what a person is condemned to without their sight, of the value of seeing, of equivalent circumstances in America, where people sue for loss of libido at the sting of an insect.

"It's a huge thing, Margaret." The poor girl was in shock, and in the habit of unselfishness. "You still haven't told me when it happened."

"A couple of days ago. John did it with his finger."

"Which finger?" I had hellish thoughts. Would the offending finger be chopped off by some retributive scissor-man?

"Oh, I don't know. He's only a child. It was an accident, best forgotten. We can't cry over spilt milk."

I grieved for the ineptness of that, for the beauty of the earth which was—perhaps only temporarily, oh pray God—divided in two for Margaret, and one half hidden.

"I can't forget it." How could I forget that my son,

no matter in how much innocence, had halved the sight of a young woman? Yet I felt guilty for the emphasis on my own pain and worry, which must be nothing to hers, and here she was behaving, as ever, so well.

"I'd rather carry on as though nothing had happened. I can drive, the doctors says, and carry right on as normal."

Was he an adequate doctor? Were not eyes sympathetic? Would she live in a slowly darkening world on account of a child's finger? Was the awful truth not that I was not happy, not pleased, but relieved, that the harm was to one eye of Margaret's rather than to one hair of John's?

Her parents must care for her as I did for him.

"Have you told your parents?" I asked. "And what does your fiancé say?"

"I'd rather keep it dark," she said, without a hint of irony.

So now I knew that the strange man was the doctor, the declarer of blindness.

"Was John with you when the doctor told you?"

"Oh, no. He sat outside with a person."

I could hardly trouble this compulsively discreet girl for further details.

I felt in those minutes so ashamed by her calmness and goodness that I wished I could offer her my two whole eyes in return for her injured one.

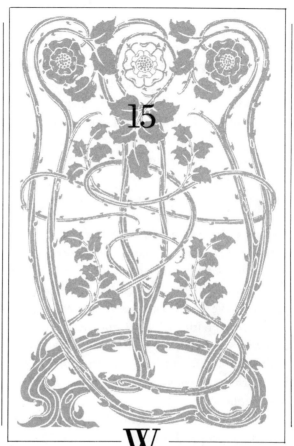

15

With my husband gone, I
had to establish a regency, John the regent and I the
protectrix. It was a household used to male thrall.
Margaret came into her own. Without her support—
beldame of the bedchamber, perhaps—I might in

lethargy simply have allowed the spring days to roll on towards Easter and beyond that to my own rolling away of a stone, the birth of the baby in late April. Sometimes for hours together I would forget Margaret's blindness; it seemed miraculously not to affect her. I could hardly understand this; several times in the night I had fallen into sleep only to awaken sharply in the dark, knowing that something terrible had happened.

But Margaret made sure that John's time was filled. The two of them were out most of the day after school, and she was busy in the mornings, with washing and ironing and her correspondence.

I was busy with my letters too. I had finished a small editing job for my friend. I seemed not any longer to have the vocabulary to remain in contact with my former life. I feared questions, the speed at which life was lived, on salary and achievement. Yet I wanted to see my old friends and for them to see John. Perhaps when they began to have children, it would happen naturally.

So when I wrote my many letters, they were almost all to people I would never meet, and at addresses of my own concoction. I was particularly touched and impressed by ordinary people. Now, after it all, I cannot imagine how I thought such a thing existed, but then I was moved to write to old dears with birthdays, children with fearful cancers, beauty queens who were Montessori teachers, even a croupière who had become a missionary. I had love to spare. I wrote to them in my comely writing on my blue paper with its repetitive address. I wrote from my fine desk, with its daily nosegay, and I created for them a world of enviable boundless grace, a letter from the blue. A letter from a person the recipient would never be confused by knowing. The letters were heavy because their paper was made of linen saturated and milled to the smoothness of eyelids and the ink of ground cobalt. They contained, on occasion, money.

Margaret took my letters with her own when she went to collect John from school. She had told me she wrote twice a week to her fiancé. She saw him at weekends and sometimes he drove over from where he worked and they met in a pub they favoured, which had, she said, a non-alcoholic cocktail lounge and a tropical salad bar. Each of them had a car which went with their job. Margaret was a fast, competent driver. When I asked her if it was really all right for her to drive, and at night, she replied, "I don't have night blindness, if that's what you mean."

The remark puzzled me, not least by its naked use of the word "blindness." If I had had an affliction, I was sure, I would be superstitiously wary of alluding to it in other contexts than its own solemn one. It was as though she had momentarily forgotten her truly blind eye, or as if I had dreamed it.

"I don't see how we'll ever do this on less than two," she said to me. She was peeling grapes at the time, to put on something she was baking. Some other nannies and their charges were expected to tea. She was referring to the number of cakes the visitors might be expected to eat. She extracted the pips from the pale grapes with the previously sterilised loop of a kirby-grip.

"What is your fiancé's name?" I asked. The question sounded rude. She moved to folding nibbed hazelnuts, soaked for a period in dilute green food colouring, into a cake mix poured from a box labelled "Creamy Dreams Flavor Release Cake."

"I call him Ronald." She did not say whether it was his name.

"Scots or Irish?" I asked. John was making handprints under the table, with the food colouring. One of those green fingers had blinded a person. I conspired with him by keeping silent. Margaret had not seen him. He was only using a tatty old jotter. I was making conversation.

"Oh, nothing like that," she said. "Not a Jocky or a Micky."

John was sufficiently absorbed not to respond to the name of the great mouse. She diminutised the ugly terms and made them sound like little puppies instead of the bad dogs of sect and race.

If she had been my equal, I would have asked her what she meant, but I thought it might appear like bullying. We are not, after all, sisters under the skin. Under the skin of us all, what you will find is fat. She might really think that Scots were drunk and mean, Irish drunk and stupid. What did that make the English? Or, indeed, the Dutch? Avuncular? Courageous? What the English were not, in Margaret's book, was black or brown or yellow. The idea of England did mean something to her, I knew, for she loved the Royal Family and would describe things as being "very nice, in the English way." She had thus described, for example, the hotel where her parents took their annual golfing holiday, in Spain. Long hair, left-wing politicians, cowardice, films in other languages, late meals, poetry, men kissing their sons, none of these was English to Margaret. Bombs were English; more than once Margaret had asked me to hire *The Dambusters* for her to watch on the video. She seemed not to think beyond these merry, bouncing bombs. In that story, the dog it was that died, being called Nigger.

"My brother is like you. He went to university. He is against the nuclear bomb," Margaret had said to me, one day when she was regretting the untidiness of the maenads camped around the local airforce base. I was flattered when she spoke of her family to me, though surprised to learn that it was only higher education which endows a person with the desire to survive.

Of course, like most people, she flinched from bombs to avoid thinking about them. The two of us probably just flinched to dissimilar effect. I could not remember having told her my opinions and suspected she deduced them from my clothes. Anyway, she and I were engaged upon the rearing of the fodder or the dropper of the undistinguished thing.

On the third day of my husband's absence, I was exhausted by lunch-time. All night I had read and wandered from bedroom to bedroom, seeking not sleep but a new confinement for my teeming body. I was reading like one starved. I progressed along two corridors of bedrooms, reading what I came across, changing books as I went. I dropped *Eros and Civilisation* for *Lady with a Lapdog*. I read too much too quickly and wanted really only to read long simple stories with happy endings. Can you think of any?

While we ate our lunch, I with Margaret and John since my husband's absence, the telephone rang. I could not move quickly. Margaret took it.

"How are you enjoying town?"

There was a silence during which she smiled as

though seeking a sweet pastille inside her mouth, reluctant, but relishing.

"He's well. Eating his chops like a lamb. Very well. Not shrinking." This last was pronounced like a verdict on a neonate—"Knot shrinking." She giggled and pulled down her jumper, soft pink bouclé, over a skirt of pastel tartan trellis. Fetchingly ready to square-dance she looked, left toe out as though stubbing an insect, cardigan hanging unentered over her shoulders, a little cape of pure pink hanging down to her—I noticed—handspan waist. She seemed to be losing weight rather fast.

John, confident it was to him that his father wished to speak, said, "I think you'll find that call's for me, Margaret."

"Cheeky," she pouted to the son of the father. My husband must have heard the soft clicks of her mouth.

"Not once. Well, once. I will if you say so. Goodbye." She handed the telephone to my bad boy.

"Yup," he said. "No prob. Can do. See you about." I heard the outrage at the other end. My husband was not accustomed to such casualness.

"OK, Dad," this in a draggy, adult sort of voice. "Lots of things. Perdita for tea. Mount raked my garden. Robert said to Margaret Mummy wasn't a chicken. I knew that anyhow. I will. I am. I do. Cheerybye."

"He says he's being good, love. Is he?" said my husband to me.

He sounded more affectionate than he had shown himself for months. I wished we were alone on the telephone. I wanted to break my undertaking to Margaret and tell him of the accident.

"I wondered if John'd like to come up, asked him in fact. If he brings Margaret. I don't think you should come; it's so dirty. I always forget." He spoke as though it were not London, capital of a fairly untormented democracy; London, where I had lived for ten years; London, where we had our house, protected by money from pestilence and the poor. But I knew he meant it for the best. He was a family man.

"Ask Horacia to make up beds," I said.

"She does things better if not asked. I'm no good at talking to her," he said. He was like that. He only had to wish for something to be done and it was. Charm, or some other white man's magic.

"That's lovely, then." It was settled. "What a time you'll have."

Perhaps this short time away would distract her from what must be her central worry. There were places to which I was longing to take John, now he was less at the mercy of small cycles of digestion and sleep. Dishonourably, I suspected they were not the places to which his father and Margaret would take him, and was pleased.

"That's settled then. I'm off to a balls-aching City thing tonight. No more loving cup apparently, because of AIDS. As if any one of those old goats was a backwoodsman. Hand in till, maybe, but not, I'd've thought, overmuch turd burgling."

I did not interrupt. I rather missed him, including his baroquely awful vocabulary.

"We all miss him, don't we," said Margaret. She served out the butterscotch whip. "I know just the coat you must wear for town, John." She notified the dreaming child of the unmetaphorical world by placing before him a dish of quivering brown dancer's belly, its jewel a pitless carmine cherry.

Her treatment of John was untouched by rancour; things seemed as they had been before.

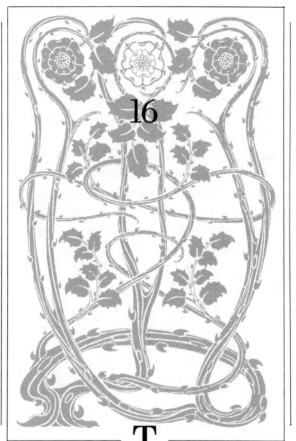

16

They left two days later, on a Friday. John had a suitcase. Margaret had two, which were epauletted like *generalissimi;* they ran on wheels.

"Even a small woman can pull them behind her

with ease," said Margaret. "Which is needed in this day and age. The English gentleman is a dying breed."

And would die shortly, if John's clothing were anything to go by, of embarrassment. He was dressed in a regulation 1920s-nursery overcoat with velvet collar, nicely piped in red.

"Don't you just love my hat?" asked its wearer. It was certainly a creation. A natty bowler in shape, its burthen was, "We're off to London town." She must have been stitching petersham all night. Like a smaller Harry Lauder, he made with an imagined cane, tipping his headgear. His eyelashes looked as though they had been sectioned into ranged clumps, the lovely vulgarity of after tears, denser yet for the shadow cast by his bowler's brim. I could not feel anything but love for him; and I felt Margaret must have absolved him of any shadow of blame for the half-blinding.

"It's detachable," said Margaret. "It just pops over the crown."

I was caught out in my squashing adult fear of bad taste and knew I was a killjoy. To make it better, I did something worse. I gave her fifty pounds, one note to avoid ostentation, to spend on herself. To avoid ostentation?

They were driven to the station by Basil. John had

insisted upon a train journey. I did not drive them because I no longer could in any comfort.

"Call me this evening," I shouted, out on the long lawn. The bunched heads of oxslips were beginning to show. No more mowing until they had flowered and gone. I realised it was a long time since I had been outside. The intense nights of undigested reading and torpid days had kept me in the house, with Edie and Bet and Margaret and John.

It was strange to be without her, stranger really than being without my son. The separation of parent and progeny was commonplace in our world. Public school? Conscription? Each forms of orphanhood. For what but death could it be a rehearsal?

It was a relief to know that it was Margaret, her very worst fault a cute way with words, who was John's companion.

I turned to look at the house, from left to right, slowly, as I did everything by now. It was of the sugary fawn brick which is friendly to the soft lichens which care only for clean air and graveyards. The shape of a lemon-quarter, the dome of the hall gently broke the bow of the façade. From the base of the dome to the ground depended four Corinthian columns, in low relief. They and the sham portico they affected to support were of gardenia-yellow stucco, the yellow deeper among the ornamentation, as the gardenia creamed to butter at its unsimple centre. Wistaria leaves, grey-pink as shrimps from the rocky-grey of their mother-trunk, were beginning to finger the house's front. I hoped some of those ghostly panacles would burst to welcome the baby.

Lead sinks stood at each side of the portico, four in all, each one containing a tall conical box tree, complementing the mazed formal box across the gravel. The box was well established and did not reveal its roots. It looked like large green toys, the four green inverted tops and the low recreational labyrinth—decorous amusement for children in farthingales and their pet dwarf.

It was fake, in fact, only fifty years old, but it pleased my husband. He did not love growing things for their vigour, but he did see a point to their capacity to flourish under discipline. Lavender, just beginning its dry intimations of heat, plumed the corners of the maze. Not to forget rosemary, which was to the garden what yew was to the park, the flinger of shade and deepener of perspective, so that things seen against it were as it were set firm against their darkness and the resinous darkness within them.

I walked slowly around the back of the house, a collection of botched Victorian innovations including several bathrooms fitted with fluted lavatories named for the family pieties: "Humilitas," "Sanitas," "Caritas." These differed in size and in degrees of impedimental ledge, rendering a long shy stay essential to ensure that the mare's tail of water had done what was intended. Men, I had noticed, did not wait. That ledge, tactfully painted with quaint scenes from blue and white oriental life (painted in occidental Halifax in a satisfying reversal of yellow men in tartan painted in Peking for the Potteries), would be scrubbed by another hand.

Bet and Edie came on that Saturday when John and Margaret were gone. The house looked so clean one could not imagine they could render it any cleaner. All housework is like that, uncumulative if done, cumulative if undone, a little like unhappy connubial love.

I was about to start on all that I had planned for that weekend alone, when there was the sound of a car arriving at the back of the house. I shut the door on my preparations, and went to see who it was.

"Hello, Daisy. I gather you're on your own this weekend. Would you like to come swimming with me? I'm off there and I've not seen you properly for ages."

"Quite a lot of me to see, too," I said, surprising myself. Mostly, I hoped the gained weight of this pregnancy would go unmentioned.

"Yes, well, it's all in a good cause, isn't it? We could even go on a regular basis." Leonora had the spare looks of a Madonna of the introspective school, translated into blondeness.

"It's kind of you, Leo, I just am so busy."

"Come off it. What with? Tidying up after the One-Eyed Monster?"

I went stiff. Who could have told Margaret's secret? What call had Leonora to be rude about Margaret?

She went on, smiling as though she'd said nothing unusual. She hooked a white lock of hair behind an ear. "Am I allowed in, or are you scared I'll huff and puff and blow your house down? Which reminds me, if I'm not going swimming, I'll have a cigarette just to make me more unfit. Incentive to swim more next time. Secretly, don't you love it when the nanny's away? You can have the babies all to yourself and eat currant buns in bed and never get up. Simon and I always seem to get pregnant when they're away."

"Leo, you're so childish."

"In that case let me in, since you seem to have stopped consorting with adults. Scaredy cat, scaredy cat." She was putting on some sort of act, I felt. Her casualness was measured.

"I won't, actually, if you don't mind. I'm just off for a rest."

"During which you'll be busy??"

"As it might be."

"Call me then, if you want anything."

She gave me a hug. I felt her light elbows on my

shoulders, the direct address of her unmisshapen body. She meant me well, I knew.

"Oh, there is one thing. Margaret's eye. Did she mention it to you?"

"She spoke of nothing but, yesterday at tea. Simon told a few National Service stories to get back at her. But it all turns out to have been a false alarm. Frankly, I wonder if it ever was. I suppose you can go blind for a bit, but well . . ." I must have stiffened again, because she smiled and said, "Rather you than me; never mind, you say she suits."

Because I did not reply to this series of small shocks and calumnies, she continued, "Still, you can have a nice weekend just pigging it a bit. We miss you. Call me if you feel like seeing us, I'll come and get you and everything, if you don't want to drive."

She was notoriously tough about other people's nannies. I was so pleased that Margaret's hurt eye had mended. Now she would have a full time in London, her sight not reduced to the margins.

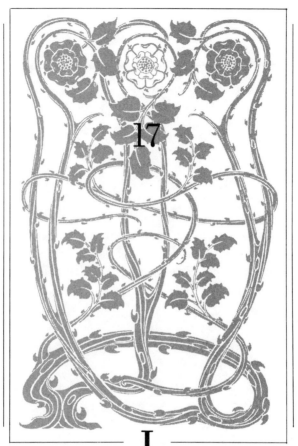

17

I did not cease to exist when they were away, but it is not of interest what the baby, whose activities were unprintable, and I, got up to on that quiet pair of days in late March. It was very calm. We took a great deal in. We grew together.

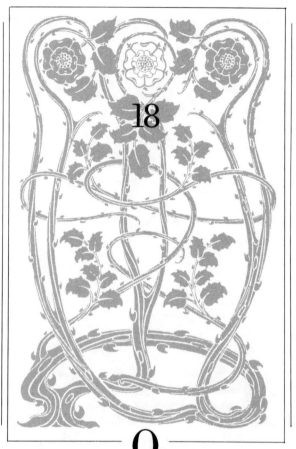

18

On the following Tuesday, I made my visit to London and to my husband. Though I longed to see him, we agreed that Tuesday was better. On Mondays I saw my doctor; besides, fish is not at its best on Mondays in any town, even a port. We always had fish when we ate together in restaurants at lunch-time. It was a custom of calcified romantic impulse, which had stayed with us.

Monday's doctor was fair of face. I preferred the other, whose job it was not to be hortatory but to perform circumspect analyses of titration and glaucometry. I could not avoid the queasy sensation that Monday's doctor, with his good profile and low handicap, felt each palpated stomach in some way a tribute to his own potency.

Give me the quiet older specialist with his conventional retort and nicely warmed speculum. I was sure that there were women who received more consideration from him than they had in the conceiving of shoesful of children. He even asked how one felt without matching action to enquiry. Performing examinations, he donned half-spectacles which made him other, and ceased to discuss the noble wines of Italy. Monday's doctor would converse socially as his hands shook each other warmly just ahent one's blushing colon. Like a dog's, his eyes were never without emotion.

Tuesday luncheon, and we were to meet like lovers, in a restaurant, not at our house, because, also like lovers, my husband had to be elsewhere at a time appointed by another. I was to return to the country by train later in the afternoon. He had some complicated and no doubt enjoyable engagement with that most absorbing hetaira, money.

We were to meet at Sweetings, a restaurant not suited to advanced pregnancy by anything but its delicious white fish and its delicious black Guinness. More than enough, taken in comfort with the beloved. Around us big boys with good skin talked all at once.

Not one had a white face. Do not misunderstand me. Some had red skin, from the tow-coloured wine sinking in the mirror before them. Some had golden skin from privately gathered sunshine. Some had brown skin, from skiing. Some were blue from an easily laid pipe of port. Two looked rather green and were not drinking at all.

My husband's skin? His skin, like that of most of those men, was the colour produced when exercise is regularly taken by a man in good health upon land whose whole horizon is his.

Although he knew many men in those crowded rooms, and some of them looked at us, wives were not visible at lunch-time in that part of London. It would be different in the areas of lighter industry—Knightsbridge, Sloane Street, Basil Street.

I had spoken to Margaret on the telephone while they were in London, each of us speaking from a house belonging to my husband. I had heard my child in the background of her voice. I had wondered who he thought of first when he woke up afraid in the night. She had sounded happy, calm, satisfied.

"Margaret is full of your time together up here," I began. It was nice that he did not take it amiss. He often seemed a little deaf. I had decided not to worry him with the story of her eye.

"And John?" He was exalted to mention his son. "Did he like it?"

"He's so like you." I smiled guiltily. I had replied before hearing the question. It was a noisy place.

"That's hardly surprising," said my reasonable spouse. Indeed, whom else might he resemble?

"Yes," I went on, "he adored it. I don't know how she carried all that loot. Is Hamleys closed due to no stock today?" I was reduced to weak jokes when tired. It kept me smiling.

"She left some of her tack at Twenty-seven, in fact. In the green room."

I wondered whether to make a sally about Margaret, and not being able to imagine her treading the boards, let alone in any green room, but my own acting career, before I found myself rescued by marriage, had not been distinguished, mostly a matter of doing other jobs while dressed as an actress. I would advise you that jobs which do not fall happily into this category are waitressing, washing-up, and nannying. Misunderstandings arise.

"But, darling," I asked him, "how will she manage without her clothes? She brought up every thread she has for that weekend."

"I don't know about these things," he said. "I make it my business not to. Though she did appear in some fairly striking fixtures and fittings, I'm bound to say. I had Bats and Cosmo and a couple of others over and they none of them acted allergic. M. was quite the little hostess. Though not the one with the mostest." He laughed and rolled his eyes at my belly.

"But she's so careful. About staying separate. Segregated, really. Like a little stranger." Whenever child care was irrelevant, she was not there. "I'd thought," I continued, tasting the silver mug and its less-cold beer as I smelled their metal and yeast, "I'd thought she was wonderful with children, not so good with people."

"But children are"—he used the voice for Churchill and very major profits—"they are"—he felt for the words—"children are little people, you know."

The little person within told its similarity to its father and knocked agreement. The large people about me suggested that he was correct, eating the food of the nursery in preparation for another strenuous afternoon of play. There appeared no crack in the smooth crescent of time which had brought them all here from there, childhood.

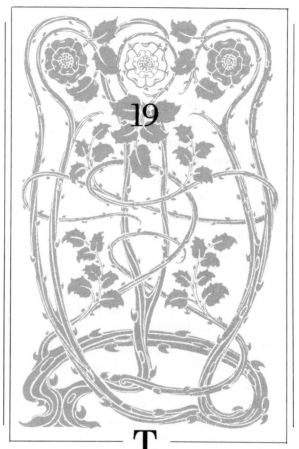

19

hen we went then we went we went." John was tired and had run out of memory but not the pleasure of its reverberation. He was in bed, clean as a clam. He had told me town tales every day after school and now it was Friday.

Each day the stories were the same; it was important not to get a word wrong. If I pretended to fluff the name of some emporium, John was affronted. His hair had been cut, by a woman who had given him a certificate and a lollipop. The old angel had gone and in his place there was a person who knew brand names and how to tip taxi drivers.

Just as I was sending letters to people unknown, I was by now making jokes to absent listeners. I had always done this a bit, but I had begun rather to degenerate.

"Give money to men who drive cabs because they are poor" had been John's words. I was outraged and, as is the adult trick, I felt I must make some kind of joke before I showed my anger. I hoped to laugh off a loss of innocence. So I released my limping joke. "Tip no further, pretty sweeting."

"I'm sorry, I don't think that's right," said Margaret. She waited for me to kiss John goodnight before doing so herself.

"I'd bow to your superior knowledge," I said, continuing my conversation with the absent listener, not actually replying to Margaret at all. "After all, you've probably read it more recently than I." I even put on a prissy donnish voice for my little put-down of the invisible joke-getter. And it is children who are supposed to invent companions.

"We had such a lark in London. Tell Mummy

about the thing the man said in the restaurant, John," said Margaret, unusually chatty.

John looked a bit shirty, then, as a child does who has heard an anecdote several times, he said, "In a restaurant where the waiters were all done up for a wedding, you'll never guess what they said. They said that I took after my mummy and they thought Margaret was my mummy because Daddy says so too. And a lady in a shop said, "Hasn't he got his mummy's lovely hair?" Margaret says the Queen went out shopping because there was no flag at the Palace. She shops wearing her crown."

Below his new feathered fringe his eyes were black as molasses. The rest of his face seemed to be stretching and modifying from babyhood to some more vulnerable because less appealing format. His complexion was changing; there were new water-stains of incipient freckle. They were the first marks on him which would endure throughout his life. In my desk I had, in an envelope given me by Margaret, the barley and sugar of his first hair. He was butting his officer-haircut into his pillow and making a cold star of creases about his head.

Were whimsy and dinkiness replacing imagination for my child, or was this merely a necessary taming? If not the Queen shopping, would it be puppets war-ring and mice in discothèques? And I actively pro-

moted ironing hedgehogs and conversational cater-
pillars.

In London, John had been bought some of those
pyjamas which presage standing up to pee and being
shy about cuddling. Twice already since they returned, I had gone into his room at night and found a
bed full of hard toys and his thinning behind escaped
from blue and white trousers woven in a neat pin-
stripe. He had not yet learnt how to tie a bow, but
insisted on doing up his own pyjama cord.

Margaret and John had visited parts of London in
which you must be a child or very rich in order to
sustain the consumption. They had eaten costly
burgers and had stood for hours in a queue to see the
newest work in wax. They had done everything that a
Middle American with a good job and no idea of
Europe would have done.

I was grateful to Margaret for her stamina and her
efficiency. She hadn't managed to fit in any of the
small suggestions I had made, and in a way I was
pleased, since that left John and me free to investi-
gate, after the birth of the baby, other Londons, before he came at length to the London of his father. I
kissed him good Friday night.

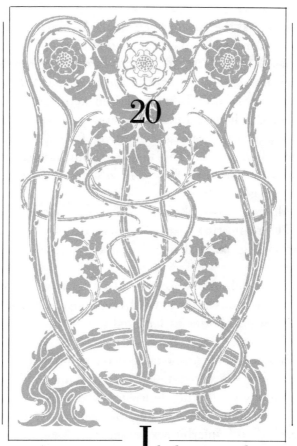

20

I had eaten, and was preparing for an evening's television. I have found that it enlivens an evening's viewing if you regard the people on the screen as potential recipients of a letter. I wasn't disappointed, though, when Margaret knocked at the door. I knew it was Margaret because she had recently taken up singing. I thought it was occasioned by tact. She did not care to interrupt me. At what she did not care to interrupt me, I did not know. In case of being surprised apparently doing nothing, I had as a child mastered a series of feints with paper and pencils suggestive of thought, industry and endeavour. This to keep off my mother, who, sure enough, went off, though in her case I need not have tried.

Margaret sang like a radio between stations.

"Come in. How nice." My social manner had gone for so long unaired that it appeared without invitation.

"I'll sit down on a chair." This, as though I customarily showed her to the Iron Maiden. My temper was getting shorter as I neared the birth.

"Do, yes. Have a nut."

Before us, on a low table of leveret-brown wood, were nuts of many varieties, each contained in a bowl of minutely differing lotus-shape, depending upon the contour of the hand of the maker. White, and brushed with unarbitrary calligraphic blue four centuries ago, these bowls composed not a millionth of the richness and discrimination which surrounded us all. They contained pecan nuts, macadamia nuts, almonds hickory-smoked and almonds dickory-smoked, teak-tree beans from the Amazon, pine nuts from Vallombrosa, and Virgilian chestnuts steeped in sugar. Nuts from *a* to *p,* fit for a night in the zenana.

But Margaret was on her diet. Of late it had been consistently maintained, and I must say she was looking trim. Always attentive to detail, she had recently, now the weather was softening, taken to shaving her legs twice a day, and to drawing a line of beige crayon around her mouth, before filling in a lightly hyperbolic bow. How did I know about the double shaving?

Bet, busy with the beautification of the baths' complexions with their especial scented abrasives, had told me, impressed, no doubt, at Margaret's industrious attention to grooming. Pregnancy is, as I say, a democratic state. People tell you things.

These warmer spring-time days, Margaret's shaven armpits were smooth and dimpled-bald as blown dandelion clocks.

Margaret's room, the pretty uncluttered room from where the farm and the church were visible, was now thoroughly the room of a modern unmarried girl. She even had a pill-tidy. I looked? I saw. Margaret was perfection, but vigilance must be observed. It cannot too often be stressed that vigilance must be observed. The custodian of your children must be as good as she appears. It was only our good fortune that she was. Her room was still heavily scented with that peculiarly sweet perfume. It overlay all other airs in

123

the room. She was good, and she, by now, almost as though we had been for her a sort of health farm, looked good too. Not mouthwatering, but very marriageable. She looked like a thoroughly passable wartime film star, nourishing. Even her ankles were diminished by diet, and, hardly ever unpropped by heels, they had something of the unferal sexiness of a troopship pin-up. Her hair was longer now and worn in a roll or a soft bow.

Her full bosom's promise was never broken, no matter how deep the V of her flowered frock or furling cardigan. Sensibly, she did not patronise a style which could be termed, even remotely, fashionable. She was a classic dresser, the undemanding and eye-easy classic of neo-Georgian, rather than the classic uniforms of my friends, the blue and white beauties. Margaret dressed as though her classical heroes were Berkertex and his legendary protector Aquascutum. Tonight, she was in her kimono, before retiring.

"They look quite good, don't they, those nuts? Have a couple," I said.

"I won't, thank you. There's many a slip twixt cup and lip." The phrase seemed loose-fitting. She spoke with care, recommencing as though I had forced her to overshoot some preordained point.

"There is something I must say." I thought of her bad eye. Was it not better, after all?

124

"What is it? What can I do? I hope it's not John?"

"No. He's a dear little boy. The image of his daddy. But . . . oh, I don't like to say."

"Margaret, what is it? Are you ill? Anything you want to tell me, do."

"I can't. I feel too bad."

"Would you like me to call a doctor? Tell me, Margaret. Nothing is ever so bad once it's out."

"I really don't feel I should."

She looked at me. I was stretched out along a sofa, hands atop the baby.

"Is it something personal? Is it something you'd prefer to discuss with your parents?" It had crossed my mind she might be having some trouble with her fiancé, and I felt it was not fair I should know before her mother and father, the policeman and the teacher.

"It is personal. There again it isn't. I mean, it's all so nice here and you are so kind and busy." She named two of my missing characteristics. She sounded like someone writing a thank-you letter for a stay in Toy Town. She looked after children, yet, being an adult, had adult preoccupations. I was worried lest I had been insensitive. Perhaps she had after all wished me to take some initiative towards friendship?

"Margaret, let me be completely open with you,

and perhaps that will help you to say what's upsetting you. We are all devoted to you. You must know that." I was speaking like a greetings card but I did want to reasure her. She was beginning, to the discomposure of her pinned hair and softly powdered face, to cry.

"Perhaps it's something you think is awful, Margaret, but I am sure I should not think so." I laughed. I almost began to tell her some worries of mine which had shrunk on revelation. I nearly told her of the inelegant bargains struck for square meals, the telephoning at two in the morning, the shoes with thin soles. Not big things, but threads leading to their black caves.

"It's so nice here. Really, really nice." She spoke with regret, as though she had no choice but to break an anthrax capsule in our attractive home.

"Yes, I think so too, but that's not the point, is it? I mean, one tries to make things nice because life is such . . ." It was fortunate that I stopped. "Hell" was the word.

"I'm afraid I have to tell you something very bad."

"Nothing is ever as bad as you fear." I sounded like a nanny. I went on. "Is someone dying?"

She did not reply.

"Is someone ill?"

She did not reply.

"Are you worried about love?" I had gone too far now, surely? I blurted, to make it less intimate, "Or, or, money?"

She winced hard.

"So it is money. Are you worried?" This was delicate country, the province of my absent husband.

"No, of course not. I'm afraid I just don't think it's very nice to talk about money."

"I'm sorry to be so unhelpful, but what else, if you are sure you are well and your family are well, and your fiancé. And John . . ." I was by now very worried. For her, of course, but I was desperate for John. I was sure that they had visited some specialist in London. John was dying. The haircut was preoperative. The garish treats were his last taste of simple fun, such fun as children are due. And I had sneered. I thought of him, sweet and shaken-down now, heavy and light as chestnut flour, the faint bright paper stars on his ceiling.

She began to shake and weep.

"Jesus," I said, "Is it the child? Is it John?" I did not stand, for fear of upsetting her. My voice was under a control which tightened all my chest and its foolish milky weight.

"Not as such," she said, mildly. Perhaps she knew to talk calmly to deranged people.

I was trying so hard not to be cross. "What as such, then?"

"It's something . . . just something . . . you ought to know."

Somewhere in the room my breathing settled. She was going to tell me that my husband saw tarts. Poor silly girl.

"If it is anything personal, I ought not," I said, furious instantly at having shown her there could be anything.

"No, no, nothing like that." She even smiled.

"What then? What, Margaret?"

"Bet and Edie . . ."

What could it be? Did they read her letters? Borrow her clothes? Eat her Diuretic Rhubarb Aero?

"Bet and Edie came into my room."

"And?"

She looked surprised that I should ask for worse than the fact of entry.

"And what did they do there?" Shred her garments, put razors in the scales, pump the toothpaste tube with glue?

"They cleaned it. But I clean it for myself."

"I think they must have wanted you to come back, to come home to, a nice clean room." We were back in Toy Town.

"But I don't like the hint I don't keep it nice myself," she wailed.

And that was that. Time of the month, I reflected, having missed nine such times.

I was rinsed with anger at myself for at once assuming her own preoccupations identical with mine.

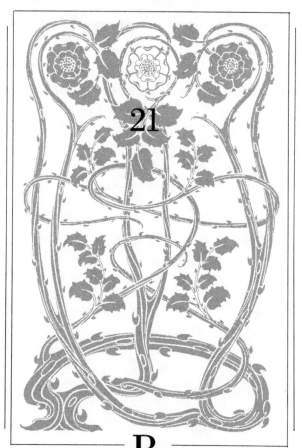

21

By the time Margaret was soothed, the television was offering only a good film. I would have preferred a bad one. I did not think I could fancy any more suggestive dialogue. I felt as though I had collaborated in the trumping-up of a charge. The whole thing had been oddly artificial. Margaret even seemed, in retrospect, to have dressed for effect. But that was not fair of me; she was simply flesh-coloured, untinctured, and I wasn't used to it. She had been wearing her scent, though, or perhaps it had become part of her? She had been so upset that at the corners of her mouth dense little cuckoo-spits of froth had formed. These were whiter than her teeth, and she nicked them away, one, two, as though it were a regular, unconsidered, aspect of hygienic maintenance. Who does not look out for the eventual destination of such flocci? Consider a quantum cotton bud and speak with a straight face of lost wax. I can't believe you have never wondered how many pounds of this, pints of that, each of us lays on the burdened earth in one quick life. Think of the secret deposits, under things, in linen, in silk, in cotton, in tissues. And then in the living tissue, too, you place deposits, if you are, as you may be, a man who does not sleep with corpses. There are men who don't.

Margaret used a paper handkerchief, drawn from the sleeve of her kimono, which at the same moment fell a little open. A lilac nightdress and her two legs were submitted to my eyes. She must have been occupied in her mind about Bet and Edie's visit to her room (why both of them?), for her legs were not, I remember, new-shaven.

That, later, as I lay in the night's first bedroom, relieved me. Perhaps she was settling in, letting go a little. Her time with us so far was already almost a quarter of John's life. She would never not be part of him.

I picked up the first book of the night. I read with only anatomical attention. My eyeballs were taking in, refracting, rotating and reassembling the images of the words. Whichever organ takes in their sounding aroma was doing so. But my fancy, unleashed from my imagination, which was obedient to the books and kept to heel, turned and turned about, trying to flatten a place among the whispering grass for myself and my baby to sleep.

My fancy began in its old hunting grounds of love, and took the scent from there.

The first book I had taken up was . . . or would you rather guess? Each of our guest bedrooms contained books chosen for it. There were standing orders at two booksellers; their proprietors could read your house like fishermen selecting flies for a river.

Our own bedroom contained the Bible and whatever yarn my husband was reading. He enjoyed true adventure stories and brave tales of butchery. A thin book, unread usually, and indicative of esoteric learning to all but the learned, would lie at my bedside, changed like the flowers.

John's room contained all the books from my

childhood, not all of them yet comprehensible to him. There were the books about shopkeeping cats and pleasant lands of counter-pain, and the books for older children about walled gardens and maid-servants sent hot chocolate by rajahs, made fairytales by time to all but a very few readers. Margaret had collected a good library of books which were composed of a cardboard cover and a cassette tape within.

The six bedrooms I slept in that night were:

The White Room, in which long-married couples were put to sleep. The Yellow Room, in which happy lovers, long married, were put to sleep. The Pink Room, in which solipsists of either sex were put to sleep. The Dressing Room, in which tired belles or young bachelors were put to sleep. The Tulip Room, in which the truly tired were put to sleep. The Explorers" Room, in which the brave slept.

As my habit had become, I would go from room to room, not entering the sheets, sleeping on top of the beds, selecting and reading and forgetting the books, like an examinee who is too late to start learning. So, that night, my fancy took me to thoughts of love, and to thoughts of him with whom I was living happily ever after. I shall tell you the story as it told itself to me as I read those other stories. You must not mind if the telling is affected by what I read as within me the old story told itself. Perhaps you can even tell me what the books were.

Arrived at a moment in my life which must be considered by all prudent persons a great opportunity for a young woman, and launched into the higher society of my now native city, I, with my inward consciousness of a painful past, but no presentiment of a troublous future, did, when the sun of attention from young gentlemen, or the cooler light of criticism from contemporaries of my own sex, became too strong, try to run away from my own shadow, which I perceived was at once too insubstantial, too large, too quixotic and too ungiving of relief when most I needed its shade. The oyster's pearly mouth now open, its temptations revealed, I wished the tide to take and rock me and wash from me all that had been, uncertain impulses, painful secrets, and lift me to the wondrous aerial land of the West. I sought one from whom in death I would not be divided.

I found him. He moved among men, men distinguishable from the rest of the crowd by a family likeness, which cut across all differences of age or appearance. His coats looked better cut. His sheets were embroidered with large monograms. His nonchalant glances reflected the quietude of passions daily gratified; behind his gentleness of manner one could detect that peculiar brutality inculcated by dominance in not overexacting activities. We entered a marvellous world where all was passion, ecstasy, delirium. A misty blue immensity lay about us. We exchanged vows.

Fear is a very big thing, and there's a great variety of kinds. I think that I had them all. So when I met so handsome, so milord, so very dressed, such a man as I had dreamed of and he confessed on several occasions to some sort of fear, *Honi soit qui mal y pense,* as the blue ribbon unwinds it. In that he could be afraid of himself, his fear was sweet to me. We were the best thing that either of us had ever known. Came John. What in the world was our connexion but this love of the child who was our duty and our life?

By now, every man we knew had a wife.

But let it remain a caution, for all those who contemplate taking small children out in small boats on the open water, that decking should be enclosed with a double row of guard-railing, firmly netted. In heavy weather, the child must be made fast in his bunk with a lee-cloth.

In case you don't speak Dutch, I'll leave out the Dutch books I read. Two lips sealed.

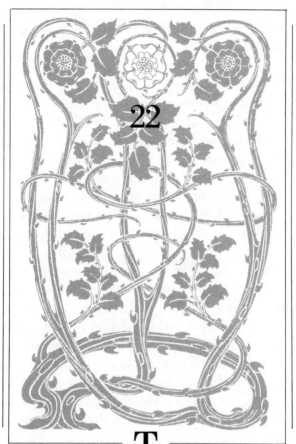

22

The books John cannot yet understand are the Dutch ones. He, unlike me, is not bilingual. My Dutch came before my English. It was my first language and it is the language in which I cook best. It is good for the nursery too. Rhymes which sound silly in English sound very silly in Dutch. Its farmyard noises are like chuckles even before the story has reached the farm gate. Is it because no one takes Dutch seriously that it has such a richness of baby-words? Dutch uncles or not, Dutch families are good places in which to grow up.

Mine was only half Dutch. My English mother waltzed off to Vienna, bored by Amsterdam.

Like women, the Low Countries are used to invasion. Also like women, they are overborne not only by men but by something even less personal and much more devastating: water. Women are eroded by the moon, Holland by water. Great facelifts of polder hold off corrosion a while.

When Holland took Empire, she was accused of shrillness, nagging, mental cruelty and bad food. Retrenched, almost uncolonied, colonised briefly by the hated Nazis, she is now a mysterious nation, open, fair, resourceful, rich, decent. What is mysterious about that? Precisely those balanced virtues in a less balanced world. How do they do it, maintain civic virtue? They are accustomed to seeing their very rich Queen on a bicycle. They are an unenvious race. Is this because of their wealth? No. The British, even the rich ones, drink envy with ice and a slice. Is it their long bourgeois past, attested to by calm paintings of doctors, advocates, ladies at carpeted tables? Is it their religion with its civilised Imitatio Maris in

137

the roar of the organ, rigged schooners six feet long, up in the rolling vaults of the Grote Kerk, hanging up there with the calm chandeliers?

Is it the light? Living within that enormous painting, the sky of Holland, the Dutch know that life is not still nor nature dead. They all partake of the same bread. In all flat lands, the sky is bigger.

They understand light, a Dutchman having developed the abutting glasses which can spy space outer and space microscopic. They have painted it again and again, so still you wait for the plushy first boughful of snow to fall at the next move of a brown fur boot, for the noise of a striped petal making its disconnection.

They made and lost the formula for that mauve glass which shows to the family at ease the canal without but shows to the observer on the bridge over the canal nothing within, though he is surrounded by clear air. All he sees in the mauve window is mauve water, mauve houses, his own mauve face on a short mauve bridge over the mauve canal. He sees a scene of mauve lustre.

From inside, the burgher sees his city, not mauve, but all the colours man sends. It is in the museum the observer will be able to see *Lawyer and his Family at Ease in their House Overlooking the Canal.*

The food, too, must steady them. No English jokes, please, about carrying ballast low. You may be thinking of the Germans. Dutch, not Deutsch. Dutch women, I can say this in modesty having an English mother, are often beautiful. In their allocation of racial dainties they have gold or silver hair, good teeth, small waists, clear blue eyes and a hint of gusto. The men, often plain, are used to pretty women so they understand courtship.

Why did my father stay in the same house after my mother left *slagroom met chocolade* for *schlag Sahne mit Schokolade?* A lawyer, full of Latin, and too prone to puns, he said it was the hook of Holland. It had him fast exactly where he was; one Amsterdam house was much like another *(Interior with Lawyer and his Daughter; Mother Absent),* so why change? We were happy, weren't we?

We had a heavy yawl, with storm keels like a seal's flippers, clumsy to handle and not very stable. Stepping its mast was enough work for two men, not a sedentary man and his child. We took buckets and darrows and caught eels inside the dykes, where the water was sweet. They hung like birdscarers in a pea field, metallic in the green water. We would trail them behind us until we had made fast to the dyke, by groaning hempen springs, so as not to tangle the lines. Later, we smoked the eels in a box my father made from the largest size of *hopje* tin. To skin an eel, imagine taking down the socks of a soaked child, swiftly and mercifully. To eat a smoked eel as the

Dutch did in my childhood, lift your head and swallow like a cormorant.

Like those ugly birds (the shag is a limber diver), the Dutch have condign and discreet skills of elegance: skating, printing and the breeding of tulips. Dutch flowers and Dutch food and Dutch books were what I had made about me of Holland in this very English England. But John (or Jan) looked absolutely Dutch, even with his cropped linen hair. At first Rembrandt's little son Titus, he had now become a Little Dutch Boy.

My Dutch tulips were grown for cutting. One whole side of the walled garden was cleaned and mulched for them. They were lifted, sorted and stored in darkness according to their age and type, and planted again in the soft days of autumn. Mount and I had found at a sale a quartet of cabinets which had contained moths (wafers of buff and silver drifting out of drawers without the panic of living moths told us this, also pins headed with brown sealing wax). We kept the tulip bulbs in these cabinets. We had lined the drawers with black acid-free tissue paper, best for wedding dresses too, since it keeps out the cruel light. Mount liked the fussing over the tulips, but Basil preferred his vegetable kingdom.

The first year the tulips came up, Mount said, "I never liked proper tulips anyroad." These tulips were improper. They squared up no smart formations of cardinal red and Sunday School pink.

Some of the tulips were very tall; some were white and green as ice, with dark brown pollen smelling of Douwe Egberts coffee. Some, shorter, twisted a little to offer torn white frills of ragged, overdressed but formal skirt. We planted each type of tulip in a block, with a thin gully between each, like paint in the pans of a paintbox. Every one of the tulips being white or cream or unsalted-butter yellow, with a fringe or a dash or sport or streak or eye or ripple or stipple or freckle or mane or dusting of one other very clear colour, or combination of clear colour, so that colour was pricked with colour.

We cut them only when all five stamens were visible. I changed their water three times a day, discarding it when the oxygen had left. I kept the flowers until every petal had fallen. I did not pick up the dropped petals until they had turned through translucency to transparency, to lassitude. The streaks on the whitest of the tulips were the red of Bols redcurrant gin, bloodless singing red. After the petal's fall, they turned very slowly through mauve to deep veinous blue.

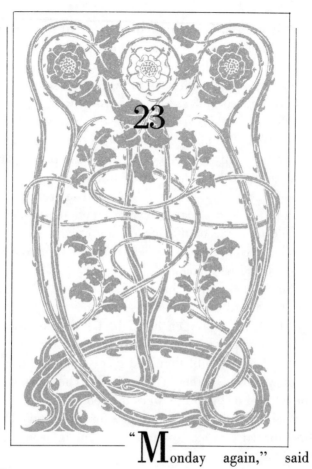

23

"Monday again," said John.

"You could call it something else," I suggested.

His shoes were on the correct feet. He was getting old more swiftly than I was, just for a time. At some point we would be level, then he would be indulging me and teaching me to ride my wheelchair.

"A rose by any other name," said Margaret. She looked quite mended. I said so.

"Was she cracked?" asked John. A wisecracker, like his grandfather.

Margaret began to bustle. She was in a hurry. Her make-up was done to a less high finish than usual.

"Meeting the other nannies?" I asked her.

She shook her head, lips pursed. I was packing a red plastic lunchbox. Red apple, chunk of Edam cut like a clog-toe, tub of yoghurt with cinnamon, two Speculaasjes biscuits in the shape of windmills. It was John's first morning at his new school.

"Eat the sails off the windmill one at a time and only if you have finished the other stuff," I told him. I had bought a chocolate *j* to give him when he got back. Zwarte Piet leaves these chocolate letters in the clogs of good children on Sinterklaas, the feast of Saint Nicholas. Not Old Nick but Fat Nick.

Margaret was revving the car. She regarded her mouth in the driving mirror, lifting her chin as though settling a stock. I saw her nick the corners of her mouth with her index fingernail, and wipe that finger on something. It was as though she did it to widen her smile. She then rolled down her bottom lip, and I saw her scoop along inside it with the fourth finger of her right hand. She wiped that finger too.

She leant on the horn.

"Bye, Mum," said John. "If you can't be good, be careful."

The car wrote the thousand thousand names of God on the gravel with its clenching tyres.

One more letter. Perhaps a reply to one of my fan letters. I liked to think of them as fan letters. It gave an eighteenth-century silhouette to my picture of myself and my correspondents. There I sat at my desk, enceinte but nimble-wristed, quilltip to well of ink, pelisse becomingly tied. I could imagine the recipient of my letters, a lady poised in the application of a mouche, the infant growing strong enough now to bestride his ribboned hobby horse, the gentleman quizzing histrionically, one hand flung beneath his coats and out, as though shaking off the dust of the street.

The letter ran:

"Dear"—it gave my name—
"Your tapes are in. We regret to inform you that Human Kindness is out of stock. Stark Mad, Arcadia and Ecce Homo are in. Yours truly, M. Cabally."

Junk mail, by any name. But who could they have confused me with? Who could possibly be interested in pretending to be me? What had I to offer the disciple of Ecce Homo?

Edie and Bet came. There was no sign that Margaret had mentioned her worries to them. Had she really been trying to express something else? Very shy or very conventional people could use these codes. Was I too wrapped up in the baby? Was it too wrapped up in me? Women all together could affect each other like small moons. Did she feel somehow excluded from the coming excitement? Did she feel she was not part of our family? She was after all so young. Love was demanded from her, yet never too much. She had to mother, without being a wife. She could never receive the sum of love given to parents. How good she was—though not good enough to eat.

"Just off," said Bet, stamping in to my morning-room. "I came to give you this, only I did not want Madam to see."

There had been this sort of jealousy between Bet and a nanny before, because Bet so loved John she wanted him to do messy things with her, tarnishy brass-cleaning and wild hooplas with suds and sopping laundry.

"All part of growing up," Bet said. "I don't reckon much to growing up without a bit of mess. Got to eat a peck of dirt before you go."

Bet had brought me a white knitted shawl, a soft wheel of web. She had made one before John's birth, too. Made for the entanglement of those pink starfish baby fingers, but warm and soft.

"It's really lovely. Thank you, Bet. You shouldn't have. You said I'd have cause to thank you and this is it. Thanks so much."

"I'd rather far give you the big thing to thank me for but I dare not, God help me, for I don't know myself what's going on." There was a cold pause. "Well, you can't stop being sweet on babies, can you?" she said. Then, not enduring my forbearance, she said, "No, but really, don't tell *her.*" This last in a demon-king whisper.

I began the soft answer which turneth up wrath to a rolling boil.

"Needs must when the devil drives. I've got to get back and feed the guineas," she said, seeping reluctantly into a normal voice.

I would not condone gossip.

Margaret must have her own reasons for objecting to an unexceptionable white woollen baby shawl. I would respect those reasons.

"How many guineas at the moment?" I asked, feeling fraudulent at the borrowing of her familiar term.

"Three," she said.

I laughed too much, as I did at private jokes

146

shared with my invisible companion before that birth.

"Gordon Bennett," said Betty. I could no longer control my laughter, at this offbeat literary attribution. "Takes you that way, does it? I couldn't stop crying myself, when I was fallen."

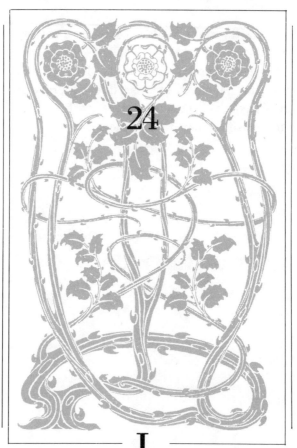

24

I was so close to confine-
ment that I had to visit Monday's doctor every
Wednesday, too. Fair of face he was, and he seemed
to have far to go as well, for today he was togged up
in enough outdoor gear to go trapping geese at Gan-

der. When I left home for the clinic, Margaret was still out; she liked the odd mystery, so we did not utterly know her life.

"All's well?" he asked.

"Yup," I replied, giving no entry for his fingers of concern. He said the Christian name of my husband in an interrogative tone.

"Yup."

"You? In yourself?"

In whom else?

"Yup."

"I'd like to talk with you about baby. He's coming any day now. The second's almost always early. He'll be happiest with a happy mother. Are you?"

"The mother? Certainly."

"This joking, Daisy, it's got to stop. Have you always been depressed?"

I could not reply. I didn't have the answer ready. He saw this and he moved in. Being a sportsman, he understood the tactics of pace. He had time. I was a private patient.

"I think you may have a few problems there. Nothing too grave, don't misunderstand me. Nothing diet won't put right."

Eclampsia? Placenta praevia? I was waiting. It turned out to be none of them, none of Lucina's foes.

He cleared his throat, as though to signal a change

of subject, and nipped up his trousers with too clean hands before sitting down.

"I hope you won't feel I'm breaking a confidence if I say you are *in loco parentis?*"

"I think the world can see I'm *in loco parentis.*"

"It may well be partly my fault."

"Hardly." Surely, no matter how flirtatious his manner, he hadn't fathered the baby? He misliked that hard tone of mine, I saw. He made retriever eyes and a soft mouth at me; no hard pads in this surgery.

I looked at the height—weight chart up on the wall. It advertised a natural and delicious-tasting laxative named Enobarb. I thought of burnished thrones, and put aside the thoughts. The trouble with having an invented companion was that they never said no to even the weakest offering.

"You are *in loco parentis* to"—I didn't interrupt him— "Margaret Pride, are you not?"

"Yes, though she's not a minor. But we'd take care of her if she ever needed it."

"If ever?" He had a serious look, whose sincerity his good looks threw into doubt. "You mean she's not told you?"

"She knows she can tell me anything. What is it?"

Again I felt the foggy despair of the night when Margaret had raised spectres and then shown them to be only old sheets.

"Daisy, you are bright but dim. If she's not told

you, it's worse than I thought, but I can't possibly tell you unless she authorises me. Call me tonight."

That "authorise" told me we were in the big world. But the counterfeit lust was back in his eyes. I agreed to call him that night.

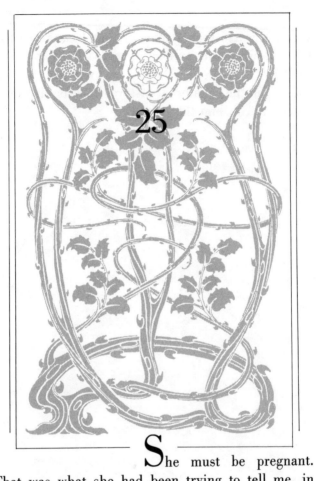

25

She must be pregnant. That was what she had been trying to tell me, in other words. Why had I not just taken her in my arms and helped her to cry? Had Betty been trying to tell me, in the morning? Of course she had. Poor

Margaret, until she knew what was to become of her baby, she could not begin to acquire its small clothes. How terrible an upbringing which does not allow the expression of simple things directly.

I drove home, the discomfort of the wheel against my high belly properly distracting and solid against my vague fears for Margaret. All the way home, through the freshly ploughed madder purple fields and the grey-lavender of copses in bud, I was making speeches to Margaret. I must not ask her why she had concealed the pregnancy.

She was not after all accustomed to free discussion. To listen to her was to hear language strangled at birth. Oh, not that. I would adopt the baby, care for it, whatever she wanted.

I went immediately up the back stairs to the nursery kitchen, taking the day's second post as I went. I couldn't run as fast as I wished. I began to call her name. She must be in the house. The outside doors had all been open and she would not have left it empty. I ran along the landing. The front stairs were carpeted and sleek. I enjoyed my own high pregnancy as I trod. Through the cusp of lunette over the portico I saw the slowly swaying green of the poplars' flames. Soon I should have a brood of children. All that luck, and poor Margaret—

The fall was not bad. It served me right for continuing to wear party shoes with my jeans. It was just that my feet seemed the only recognisable part of me, so I rewarded them with shoes.

The heel of the right shoe snapped off halfway down the front stairs. It lay there like a glassy clue. I twisted and fell to the bottom from that point. I hit first my coccyx then my belly against the two lowest banisters, which stood on the last curves of the glacier of pale wood which was our staircase. These final banisters were cast in bronze, plunder from a greater house. Bound in brazen unthinking reeds, their strong poles bore the fasces, two green-gold double-headed axes.

They were the reason we never let John use these stairs.

I couldn't move. I lay. When I had collected some breath I spent it all on a yell. I yelled her name. I hoped I was not frightening John. If she were not here, he could not be. I thought I could hear the radio, a man and a woman in unconvincing loveplay. Poor girl, how lonely she must be, to omit to turn off that machine. She must fear silence.

I stopped yelling when I realised I made no sound. I decided to be calm. I wasn't uncomfortable. I counted the knots on the underside of the rug which I'd flipped over like a ray's fin in my fall.

She got me upstairs. I do not know how she did it. She said she must have been in the garden when I got home.

I remembered at once that there was a thing about which she wanted to talk to me. Soon I would remember what it was.

I was in my bed, but, like a drunk, not dressed to be there. I was in the clothes of my fall, stiff maternity jeans, hard blue sweater. Margaret was reading at my bedside. At the foot of my bed small pillows were laid in a clutch upon the chaise-longue; its silk was stretched tight as though for tanning. The white sun flayed a heap of papers at the bed's end. Some of them were cornered with gay paper squares. They had some message for me which floated just out of reach, slipping away from me down the next wave.

Some of the small pillows were the shape of Chinese lanterns, or seedheads, and two were "bone pillows," the softly quadrilateral shape which rests the neck or the toppling belly. The last time you need pillows, when you are bone. Margaret was right to discard the pillows; they were the last thing I needed.

Her book was *Patience Rewarded;* its cover showed a couple embracing between a large house and a large car. She was small and he was big. Poor Margaret. Even her books were low in calories, and puffy with synthetic sugars. Still, I could see she was enjoying her reading. I watched her, soothing myself with the pretty sight.

"Well done, you had a nice sleep," she said. Hurt,

I was a child, and she spoke to me as though I was her charge. I was still feeling for the thing I must say to her. I was sore, but I did not want to burden her with that. I knew there was some reason I should be tactful to her. I lay for a time and did not sleep, watching her, slight and poised, in my old nursing chair. She was so small its truncated legs did not make her awkward on its low seat.

The room had been emulsioned before the war, the yellow of coltsfoot. Chafed in places, the old paint sucked in light as chalk does water. The ceiling's rose was a plain wreath of white apples upon white boughs. Dropping white muslin in a tent over our bed, crossed double axes of gilded pear wood surmounted the four pillars between which I sprawled.

Margaret, on the low chair, its cambric cover tied like a pinafore behind, fitted in, as she had since the first day. She put her book to the floor; it had no spine to snap as she splayed it.

"You fit in so well, Margaret," I said. I was reluctant to nick the silence. "Is that John I hear?" I heard nothing, in fact, but I wanted, without appearing to question her care, to know where he was. I wondered how his first lunch had been.

"I gave him to Lizzie for the afternoon. There are some betimes chicks in the partridge pens and Robert says they feed well from children." She was using Robert's country phrases easily.

She thought of everything. But whose was he to "give"? When had she done this? Before or after my fall?

"Did you meet the other nannies?" I asked. I was surprised by how it hurt to talk.

I knew the look she gave me, but not from her face. I remembered it from the face of my father when he tried to make my mother's total disappearance another nursery absence, as though she had just gone to fetch a pail of water or to pull out a plum.

"Aren't you getting on with Jackie and Sue and the others?"

The pain made me careless of the courtesies.

"Oh, they're fine. It's not up to me." I knew that the best friendships shifted now and again, changing with weight lost or admirers gained.

There must have been some teasing over the love-shot keeper. But could that be enough to cause the severance? I remembered the poor girl was pregnant. Nannies must be able to tell immediately. Look at Margaret, with me. After all, they worked with the animals. A pregnant nanny. She was condemning herself to invisibility.

"Is there something you would like to tell me?" I seemed recently to have asked the same question.

"No. I couldn't. I couldn't." She twisted her wristwatch and rotated the pearls at her earlobes. Dated, womanly signs of distress, learnt no doubt from mother and from screen.

"Is it something about yourself?"

"I can't say."

"I think I can guess. Do you want me to say?"

"Oh, no." It was as though I might spoil something. Already the progressive slow waltz of mother and foetus had begun between Margaret and the child she carried. She did not want me to make her lose the beat.

"Margaret, are you in trouble?" I do not know where the phrase came from.

"No. It's you." Well, I knew that. She and the handsome doctor must both think me very dumb.

"Try talking to me, Margaret. Try, love." My back was burning, slowly, like lit gun cotton soaked in spirit. My skin was smoking to crackling with the heat of the pain.

"I'd rather not, if you don't mind. It isn't nice." Her eyes filled with tears. So, she had got a child, but had not enjoyed the getting. Was it Robert's? Was it the child of Ronald who was neither Scots nor Irish?

"Is it something I could help with?" After all, she had said, "It's you." What did she mean? Did she feel trapped in our rich life, was there something we had not done?

"It's quite natural, you know," I said, exhausted with diplomacy and pain.

"They think so."

"They?"

"The other nannies." She might as well have said "navvies." I heard the contempt in her voice.

"Weren't you planning a night out soon? A birthday? Dawn's? I seem to remember something of the sort."

"I've had to tell them I can't go."

Could there really be no comradeship among women? I was sure the father's friends must be drawing shoulder to shoulder, buying him drinks, congratulating and commiserating. Like eels or alligators, women move over each other, ruthless and unimpressionable, rushing for the warm seas of mating and rearing.

"Don't let yourself be hurt by what other people say," I said.

Again she said, "It's you."

I was losing patience.

"You'll have to explain. I'm lost." The pain in my back reached round and keelhauled me. I was drawing out Margaret, and my guts were being drawn out of me.

"It's what the other nannies say."

"About me? Come on, sticks and stones."

That was a bit prissy of her, really, if loyal. Surely they all discussed us at scurrilous length? Why should she object? We took on their attention in remunerating their labour.

"Not you, as such."

I was now in real pain. I knew it from somewhere, though it seemed fresh. In the air I smelled the bubble of blood you smell before a big fight. My forehead was cold with sweat. Something I could not prevent was expelling myself from me. I began to breathe very carefully as though I were hiding from someone who sought my life, behind only the thinnest of curtains. This pain had a familiar face, but its expression was twisted. I did not want brutally to ask her how pregnant she was. I did not care to hurt or scare her.

"Have you rung the doctor?" I asked. I knew he had something to do with all this.

She regarded me swiftly and said, "No."

Then, as though in alarm, she continued speaking, maybe to ensure my silence. She appeared terrified at the mention of the doctor. She smelt, suddenly, of acetone. The sockets of her arms were circled with sour cloth. Her lips showed white gums.

I knew then that I was struggling for the life of my child.

"I can't see those nannies any more. They say it's

your doing he loves me. He loves me. And so does the child you call your son. He loves *me.*"

There being no doubt who he was, I felt with no shock the waters break from me into his bed.

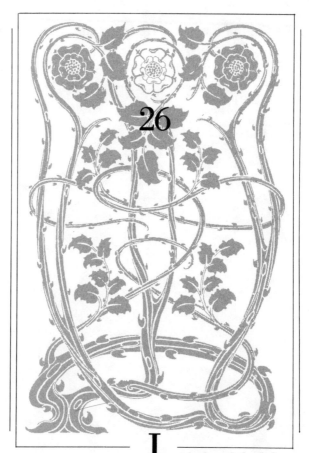

26

I said that I had love to spare. That happens when you have a child. There must always be more. Not more of everything, but more of love. You never know when it may be needed.

It was easy to love my beautiful son. I had not found it easy to love Margaret. I did not even like her. I romanticised her because I wanted a quiet life. I thought I did like her because I needed her services. Doing this, I put my child in the care of a scheming fantasist. Most galling, it is the smallest things, and the things which make me despise myself the most, which I mind worst, to this day. I did, while of sound mind and with no particular job to do, allow my son to be defused, disconnected from what is important, alive and funny. I allowed him to be taught not only the natural sins of his fathers, but those sins glorified by their victims. Margaret believed in granite-jawed potentates; men who were men were the men for her. Not as they were, but all cleaned up. Nannied. Lightly castrated, like princes in the ballet.

Poor Margaret. She would have been scandalised if she'd known of wet-nurses. Bottles only, please, and not of gin. No jugs, no dugs.

Why did she care for children? Why work with the animals? I still wonder, and can only think that it was the opportunity to participate in the books she'd read and the films she'd seen. These are the books read and the films seen by most young women, but very few have decided to become a pearl. And Margaret was a pearl, of very great price.

I spoke of the hingelessness I wanted for my son,

a life seamless and uninterruptible. But I was wrong. It is for those people I now fear the most, for, when the blow comes, they are unhinged. It is better to have a little grit, a slight abrading. That is what life actually brings, if not worse. The perfect ovine smoothness encloses the lives only of the very stupid or the very ill. We give it to our tiny babies until they are accustomed to a little rocking.

Until that time we shelter them against even the slightest swell. Margaret had swallowed the bait whole; she believed in the calm green sea of money. It rocked her, having sung her its songs (Ecce Homo, *Patience Rewarded,* and the countless other siren tunes), and then it wrecked her. Unresourceful, pusillanimous, bled of initiative by the long cold wait for the handsome prince, she had neither wish nor wit to build herself a shelter of the wreckage.

I was all but wrecked too, for I was beginning to roll with that beguiling ocean, and it would have pulled me down as surely as it buoyed me up.

John and the baby at least made landfall.

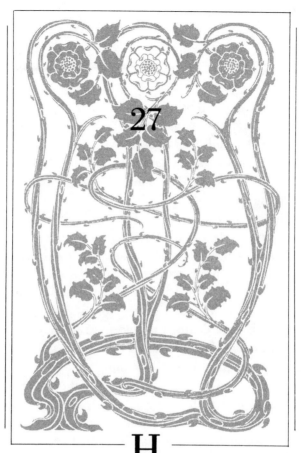

27

Have you ever seen books burnt? The idea is vile; the fact is worse. There is no excuse for it but a new Ice Age. The only excuse for pyres of books is a killing need for warmth.

The wreck made of our lives, whose chapters were so ordered, whose bindings so handsome, title and verso so clean and clear, was made by such a need in Margaret.

Yet in my infatuation, turning the pages, engrossed in plot, enamoured of surface, I could not read what I had eyes to see.

Burnt books leave scum, not light ash. The gum of cows' feet, the sea-bed minerals, are leached out. Only the twenty-six frail characters are destroyed.

The doctor relied on my seeing what my eyes told me. Never rely on intelligent people to be so. My eyes told me nothing; my nose, which should have told me something, did not.

I said I was vain, but I had not looked in any mirror I could avoid for seven months. I veiled them as though for a death. I turned from them as though I drank blood. In Sweetings I did see myself. Not, as I said, invisible, but not wishing to be seen. And impossible not to see. What could the other men have said to a man with a wife the size of a whale? For every pound Margaret lost, I put on two. In two years, the doctor says, I shall be myself and not these three selves in the one skin.

That weekend when Margaret and John Solomon were in London was a lost weekend, though you will see its scars on my green marble legs and leg-o'-mutton arms. Leonora must have sensed I was about

to do wrong. What we did together, I and my con-
script accessory to the fat, was attend a children's
party lasting twenty-four hours, a party for ourselves
alone. Seven loaves with chocolate hail, white milk
bread paved with butter and the pastel sugared ani-
seed the Dutch call little mice, mob caps of jelly and
lakes of cream, egg sandwiches for a team of
hungers, and shoals of herring, pink, silver, white,
grey, and the morbid maroon which is so delicious
eaten with warm yellow potatoes and cold soured
cream off a hot spoon.

A feast for Dutch children, you see it was. After
that, a dyke of chocolate, smooth Droste pebbles,
disks as brown as sea coal, or creamy like the best
Friesians between their mappy black. We ate truffles
rolled in pulverised Verkade until they were as
smooth as mushroom caps. I held off the sea with our
solid wall of eating, but its fingers broached our
dyke.

Having been made to feel so small, I chose to
make myself large.

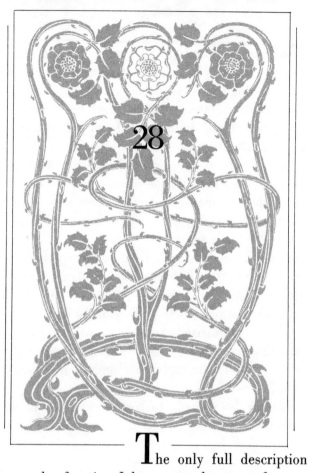

28

The only full description
of a work of eating I have served you so far was
when I described to you the blue and white bowls of
nuts, laid out after supper. Enough to keep . . .
What is it nannies say? Enough to starve the feeding
millions . . .

And that was after eating supper. Soon after Margaret came into our house, I began my secret eating. It was not easy to keep secret, but no one cared to mention it, and for a time I carried it well, like a Polynesian cannibal queen. Then again, it might have been the bulk of the new life, and no one likes to tempt fate by criticising the unborn.

Our house, that long full term of pregnancy, contained two countervalent madnesses, both to do with food.

I did not know, until the conflagration at the very end, of her miserable bringings up.

My hogging began in joy. I was a pig in muck. Not two, not four, but ten of everything. I moved with the times; I was a decimal eater. I believed in eating only the best and I made it beautiful. I contemplated its beauty before commencing engorgement. The virtue of the food, its rarity and cost, the secrecy of its preparation, the hidden expeditions mounted for it, gave my votive sessions the nocturnal glamour of a love affair. By day I cut normal sections from the pies in the larder. By night no moon of cheese could satisfy me.

Even when the fat began to heat and chafe, to require powdering between its rolls after any exertion, I felt innocent. The more innocent, if it were possible, the more I ate. The pleasure was so rich and so simple, so harmless, so uncomplicated.

Anorectics are said to fear adolescence. My glowing feasts were celebrations of being a child. I lifted from myself the weight of thought as I donned that precious fat.

The exquisite night-time sense of ceasing to be homesick for some quite fabricated home, some honeymoon of childhood, of engaging with something real and purely unreciprocal, made my eating times almost holy to me. It still seems strange that all that glory turned not to light and radiance but to heavy dullness and the shifty sexlessness of fat.

At its height, the midnight feasting was Dutch, wanting only an urn of tulips to freeze it to still life. I arranged cold fowl (which I ate, wrenching like a midwife with my hands) and sausages with flecks of white fat. On pewter dishes I dumped clouds of bread and flitches of striped speck. Transparent red smoked beef hung over plates, silky as poppy petals. I tumbled grapes from blue to yellow and the weak purple of primulas. I cushioned myself with Bries rich as white velvet. All this in trencherly quantities.

It was so beautiful; how could it do harm?

At the same time, Margaret was carrying out her inverted worship of the same god.

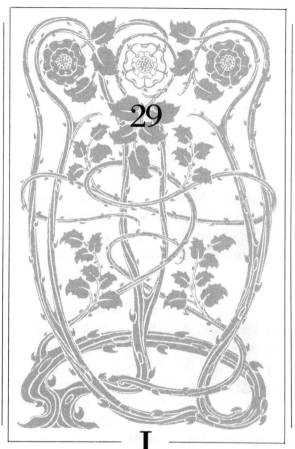

29

I should have smelt her illness. I saw only fertility, imagined only the healthy malaise of pregnancy, when the doctor tried to hint at what was wrong. She was not as ill as she had been, twice before, but each time it grew harder for her body to bear the lightness she laid upon it. To me, she looked simply rather enviably slim, because I knew I was unenviably fat. Yet by now she was weighting her hems with shot and padding her frocks with dressings; dressing up, you might call it.

I should have thought about her poor hirsute limbs, observed not only the gestures but their reasons. Thick spittle is caused by potent tranquillisers. They clog you up and wring you claggy.

Bet and Edie had been seeking the source of a bad smell, fearing rats. That was why they went to her room. But it was more than rats, which are to be expected in any house among fields and farm buildings.

In the end they did trace the smell. It came from one of Margaret's suitcases. It left with her, never having been opened. Bulimia is frequently the resort of very tidy people. She couldn't stand the mess inside, perhaps, all that disorderly digestion. She kept surgical gloves in the nursery bathroom, so she didn't get dirty hands as she put a long feather down her raw throat. She dusted the gloves with talc before entering them, John said. He was familiar with the routine, considering it part of the grown-up woman's toilette. He told me this after we'd all come back from hospital, and I asked him to powder the baby. "Why?" he asked. "Is she getting ready to do icky-poo?" The expression wasn't his own. After she had gone, I found the most silver and babyish of John's curls in a very small envelope, at the back of one of her drawers. In a way, she was a witch, though her poor spells did not snare the handsome prince. I wondered if the fiancé too was a fairy story, the reliable foil of fiction, in sharp contrast to the flashing attractions of Mr Right.

She purveyed fairytales. She believed in them too, the social lures and magic potions. Yet, without the prim wisdom of Alice, Margaret in Wonderland had not the education, the upbringing, if you like, to know when to obey the instruction "Eat Me."

I don't like the idea of all that upbringing.

John, reborn by her departure, ceased his more knowing ways and cute contrivances. Perhaps we may even hope he does not grow up to become the baby prince and ideal man of Margaret Pride, godlike, intolerant, made of brass, stupid as the Himalayas.

Would you like to borrow *Patience Rewarded?* Here's a good bit:

Condemned to be invisible, just Jamie's nurse, Elsa nevertheless took care to style her soft brown hair and slipped her creamy gown over her slight form. The neat collar and cuffs toned, she reflected, with the colourways of the Duke's own suite, where the Duchess lay, even now, hideously obese, eating, eating, eating.

A slim volume to keep you awake at night. We're none of us innocent. There's a fairy story for everyone.

Margaret wrote, too. She kept notebooks of every single thing she ate. One was left behind. It was very neat, a thin blue jotter with ruled pages. In the margin were ticks and crosses, many more ticks. They were bleeding her empty, those little red ticks.

The jotter she left behind was blue, with the fading green handprints of my son marking its cover.

Beneath her mattress (we burnt it later and the ash stayed about the farm for a windless summer week) were some of the letters I had sent out to the noble army of unknown friends, and some sheets of our blue paper. With difficulty, words as misangled as little ships in the wrong bottle made their way over it, in a stiff model of my writing. Disliking me, as she certainly must have done, she yet attempted to turn herself into what she imagined I was.

She was not taken away by her parents, the policeman and the part-time schoolteacher. She was taken away by her parents, the Irish stable lad and his dead wife.

The poor man stood in the kitchen, Lizzie told me, and he was scared of his daughter. He took a drink of tea, but he left it on the side. His legs were that bowed you could ride through them. All veins and knuckles, said Bet, that's the wind and the drink; but a nice sort of man. The kind you could tell was good with animals. She sent her dad up to get her cases. She had refused even a drop of water since the new baby had begun, so she was that weak she'd to sit in a chair. Edie had padded the chair because her bones were bruising her—she was hungry to do herself harm—and wound her elbows and the coathanger of hips with rolls of yellow chiropodist's wool, so's she couldn't hurt herself.

She'd bitten Bet, and set fire to something in her room, so Lizzie reckoned she was dangerous, but Edie said, "The poor girl thought she was bettering herself. She spoke to that father like she employed him."

The man whom Margaret had told to pick on someone his own size turned out to have been the robust but lovesick Robert, who had also had an appointment with the doctor. After it was all over, he told me that Margaret had threatened John with a beating if he were to tell me Robert had been there. "A beating?" I asked. "But she knew she was not allowed to hit John."

"No," said Robert, hot and uncomfortable. "She said you would hit him."

The thing she burned in her room was an animal.

It was a soft rabbit, as tall as John. It turned out that my husband had bought it along with all the other toys, guns, tanks and interstellar death gambits, because she admired it when they were in London.

"I thought it was the kind of thing that sort of rather ugly girl likes. Substitute for a man, something along those lines," he said. "They charged like the Light Brigade for it too."

He did not know the meaning of meanness, but he couldn't see love if it poked him in the eye.

If it is so that the fat wish to be a shadow of their former selves, the sickly thin wish to be the flesh of their future selves, not a flesh fed by nourishment, but the plump, taut, muscled and yet tender flesh of romance—ready to be carved. While they reject and vomit food, for what are these girls paying, these girls wanting to be hollow? What fantastic connection has been made between daydreams of beauty and romance and that life of bitter spitting?

How I longed to be but a shadow. I had taken myself seriously, but had not at any point taken seriously that self.

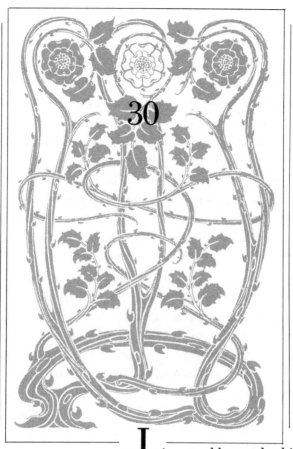

30

It is you, blue and white girls, who brought me back, who made a bridge for John and the baby over the dirty waters of that choppy time.

The baby came after two days. Margaret did nothing for the first two hours of my labour, but then my husband came home. Someone had seen Margaret's smashed car, and had gone to alert him, which was part of her plan.

She told me, as I lay in labour, that what she hadn't expected was to be completely unhurt. She had imagined that he would rescue her, having found her just a little, becomingly, blooded, winged only by her accident, and that would be that.

She did not wish to acknowledge her real sickness. She longed for the erotic violence of romance, the blood matching the lipstick, the steamy meeting of fire and ice. She had discounted me. I had given her every reason to do so.

She was strong enough to haul me from the glassy stairs where my evening slipper had spilt me because she was drunk with fury. Some sinister shreds of conscientiousness bound her. She was angry to be mobile. She had hoped, I suppose, to diet herself to beauty and to crash herself into the sights of my husband, who would then act on the love she knew he bore her.

All she did was destroy the car.

He came upstairs roaring, "Bloody nannies. They're all the same. They smash a car as soon as look at it. Stupid cow. My son could've been in that car. Daisy, Daisy, where are you? Wake up, get up,

178

the car's crashed. It could have been my son, you bitch, for Christ's sake."

I screamed and screamed, and he came to our room, and saved me, not from the pain, or the mess, but from the vituperative, obsessing voice of Margaret, who had been sitting knitting as I panted and heaved, and telling me her love story. "I am glad it's your body, not mine," she began each mad versicle, and then went on to explain why I would die if I had any sense of the proper thing to do. Her plan had not gone entirely awry, she perceived. I might yet die. She had already started taking my name; it was only a little way from taking my life. The longer I was unhelped, the better it would be. She hoped that the baby would live, and she and Solomon would bring it up as their own. It would never know that its mother was a fool, a fat fool, a moon-faced fool with her head in the air. The one thing I could do and she could not was have children, and she would take care of them. She had starved herself to barrenness. The best thing I could do was die. It was what would be most helpful. I was at such a grovelling depth of acquiescence that I almost wished—for politeness' sake—that I could. Until I felt the tug and assertion of a quite other person from within myself and knew clearly that I too had been mad and now I was fighting sane. I tried to get to the telephone, of course, but she went for my eyes with her knitting needles. They were the finest steel needles, the best for baby clothes. My eyes are fine too; needle-sharp. She didn't touch them.

The baby is quirky like me, and smiles, dreaming, in the middle of eating. I will teach her what I so painfully learnt: that stupidity is not a virtue, that others do not care the more for you if you bury yourself, that anger will out at the end. I can see already that she does not have my sin of extravagant co-operation, my perverse will to be polite at any cost.

Margaret had been the stranger whom our family could not accommodate. Though we were four, we were almost overcome by her single strength. What was the strangest thing of all? I took her in because I hated her on sight, and was ashamed of myself for doing so. When she went, so did the fear which had made my life little better than a stretched skin against the weather. Together we had turned the gingerbread house of family life into the smelt blood and ground bones of the most cruel tales.

While I was getting better my friends came and read to me, real stories about Olivia who has a garden, Katherine and her battling husband, double-crossed Viola, Helena whose husband beats her and says her love annoys him like a stone in his shoe, and Brutus's wife, who dwells in the suburbs of her lord's pleasure. Each of these stories has a hard centre.

Our daughter emerged into this world of pearls and swine, eccentric, laughing, at the heart of things. Held by her slapped satin feet, she bellowed disapproval and glee and the resolution to wear out twelve dozen pairs of dancing slippers before morning.

It is possible, without knowing it, to live at the margin of your own life. Life leaks away and you watch it go, a rope of water coiling down to nothing and the dark. It was my good luck that the tide came inshore and carried me past the shipwrecks and lost things of my former existence, and out once more into the day's eye and the loud resounding blue and white.

A NOTE ON THE AUTHOR

Candia McWilliam was born in 1955 in Edin-
burgh, where she was educated until, at the
age of thirteen, she went to school in England.
After leaving Girton College, Cambridge, with
a First, she worked for *Vogue* magazine and
later as an advertising copywriter until her
first marriage, in 1981, by which she has a son
and a daughter. In 1986 she was married for
the second time. She lives with her husband in
Oxford. Her first novel, *A Case of Knives,* was
the joint winner of the 1988 Betty Trask
Award.